Ilil Arbel

MADAME KOSKA & LE SPECTRE DE LA ROSE

A MADAME KOSKA MYSTERY

bhc press

Livonia, Michigan

Edited by Louanne M. Wheeler
Proofreading by Caren Hayden

MADAME KOSKA & LE SPECTRE DE LA ROSE
Copyright © 2019 Ilil Arbel
All rights reserved. Except as permitted under the U.S. Copyright Act of 1976, no part of this publication may be reproduced, distributed, or transmitted in any form or by any means, or stored in a database or retrieval system, without prior written permission of the publisher.

This book is a work of fiction. The characters, incidents, and dialogue are drawn from the author's imagination and are not to be construed as real. Any resemblance to actual events or persons, living or dead, is entirely coincidental.

Published by BHC Press

Library of Congress Control Number:
2018953412

ISBN Numbers:
Hardcover: 978-1-948540-78-0
Trade Softcover: 978-1-948540-11-7
Ebook: 978-1-948540-12-4

Visit the publisher:
www.bhcpress.com

Other Books by Ilil Arbel

Madame Koska & the Imperial Brooch

Contributing Author

The Mysterious Affair at Styles
by Agatha Christie
Introduction and the Hercule Poirot/Madame Koska Short Story
"The Case of the Missing Silk Evening Gown"

With many thanks to...
Louanne M. Wheeler
for her invaluable editing and proofreading,
and to the wonderful people who have done so much to
encourage me as I plunged into the dangerous
water of murder and mayhem—
Kathleen Fish, Barbara Houlton,
Sunny Gwaltney, and Penelope Fritzer.

Introduction

This book is Madame Koska's second adventure. She will once again design *haute couture* at her London atelier while engaging in sleuthing and catching evil-doers on the side. It is not necessary to read the first book, since each story stands alone, but it may be useful to give some information about the era, the styles, and the characters. If you prefer, however, you can certainly skip the introduction and dive into the plot. Personally, I have the terrible habit of reading a book first and the introduction last, since I greatly fear some secrets would be revealed, but I assure you, in this introduction I am very careful not to give you even a hint.

The book is fiction; these exciting events never happened. However, some of the organizations, and several characters as well, were based on historical material which I found fascinating and wanted to discuss. Besides, I suspect that if I don't confess, some astute readers would catch me and complain that I am deceitful and not to be trusted; I might as well come clean right away.

Several "regular" characters existed in *Madame Koska and the Imperial Brooch,* and are fictional. Those based on historical figures are:

Sasha Danilov—Serge Diaghilev

Tanya Lavrova—Anna Pavlova

Monsieur Bex—Léon Bakst (only mentioned in passing)

Victor Parizhsky—Vaslav Nijinsky

Galina Danilova—Tamara Karsinova (though Karsinova never married Diaghilev)

Michel Fokine is recognized as the choreographer but does not appear in the book.

While taking plenty of liberties, I based the *Ballet Baikal* on the sparkling, magical *Ballets Russes*. If I could indulge in time travel, I would visit some of their performances and videotape them.

L'Après-midi d'un Faune

Vaslav Nijinsky choreographed and danced this famous and controversial ballet with Diaghilev's full approval. Many of us are so familiar with it that we do not realize how revolutionary it was; the first performance created an uproar. Nijinsky had previously scandalized audiences with what they perceived as gross indecency; come to think of it, he had a reputation for shocking even his greatest admirers. But never before had he done something so extreme. It is not clear if Diaghilev knew what Nijinsky planned to do at the end of the show or even if Nijinsky planned it at all. He was already mentally unstable at the time, and so it could have been spontaneous. I suspect that Diaghilev did know and that he trusted that the sophisticated Parisian audience and critics would not bat an eyelash. He was mistaken.

To begin with, this was no classical ballet. The stage and the dancers looked like a Greek bas-relief slowly coming to life. Most of the dance was performed in profile, so the classical "positions" were eliminated. The scenery and costumes by Leon Bakst were gorgeous, but there were no tutus and not even toe shoes. The ballerinas floated about barefoot in delicate and revealing dresses and diaphanous veils. The Faun wore tights that were patterned after a dappled horse, decorated with vine clusters, and a wig with short horns. The eerie, sensual music by Claude Debussy increased the audience's discomfort.

The simple storyline is based on Greek myths and lacks a plot. The nymphs appear, dancing together and playing. The Faun observes them, proceeds to chase them, and finally tries to seize one. The nymph manages to evade him, and runs away, leaving her veil behind. The disappointed Faun climbs a cliff, lies down on the veil, and becomes immobile. The curtain falls.

Except that on that first performance in Paris, Nijinsky did not remain immobile. As he lay down on the veil, he started moving in a blatantly sexual way. After a short, horrified silence, the audience jumped to their feet, climbed on their chairs, and began screaming, hissing, and protesting; some tougher souls laughed, whistled, and applauded. It was pandemonium.

But no one could beat Diaghilev for a cool head in an emergency. As always, he knew exactly what to do, and gave an order to repeat the ballet from beginning to end. The audience calmed down and watched for the second time—and the show ended with huge, unanimous applause. Victory for Diaghilev?

Not yet. The next day, the great critic Gaston Calmette wrote a scathing article in *Le Figaro* newspaper; he accused Diaghilev not only of immorality but of presenting an artistically inadequate performance. It is worth quoting some of it:

"Anyone who mentions the words 'art' and 'imagination' in the same breath as this production must be laughing at us. This is neither a pretty pastoral nor a work of profound meaning. We are shown a lecherous faun, whose movements are filthy and bestial in their eroticism, and whose gestures are as crude as they are indecent. That is all. And the over-explicit miming of this misshapen beast, loathsome when seen full on, but even more loathsome in profile, was greeted with the booing it deserved."

Calmette was answered by the famous sculptor, Auguste Rodin, who not only loved *L'Après-midi* but was also a personal friend of Diaghilev. The controversy spread, and Paris was divided into two camps.

The newspapers went on with many articles—and the result was a huge financial success for that season since everyone had to see it.

Anna Pavlova

When Pavlova first auditioned in 1899 at the Maryiinsky Theater at age eighteen, the famous ballet master Marius Petipa could not believe his own eyes. He later said that throughout his entire long career, he had never seen a ballerina perform quite like Anna Pavlova. He hired her on the spot and felt his action was justified since she became an overnight success. Pavlova went with Petipa to many countries in Europe, became the Maryiinsky's prima ballerina, and everyone expected her to stay there for her entire career.

But Pavlova had little loyalty to her old benefactor. In 1909 she unexpectedly joined Serge Diaghilev's *Ballets Russes* and went to Paris with him. She was as great a sensation there as Vaslav Nijinsky. There is almost a mythical element in the story. How could the two greatest ballet dancers of all time be at the same place and at the same time? How could such a coincidence happen? It seems impossible—and yet it did.

Pavlova did not return to Russia but did not stay with Diaghilev, either. This seemingly delicate creature had a mind of her own, and she would not have anyone manage her career and dictate to her when and where she would dance; Diaghilev was too domineering despite his charm and wanted everything done his way.

She became a nomad and traveled all over the world on her own. She appeared before royalty but did not disdain modest dance halls, either. While royalty admired her, she also performed at second-rate theaters, sometimes as a part of a show that included jugglers and animal trainers. No matter what the stage, she always danced as if possessed by a power higher than herself, and the audience would gasp at the dark, exotic elf that seemed to make time stop as she danced. She made the dance look so easy; it seemed as if it cost her no effort at all. No one guessed that her muscles hurt constantly and that she had herself wrapped with tight bandages when she was not dancing. Her name was recognized in every continent.

In 1931 Pavlova planned to dance her famous solo of "The Dying Swan" at a royal command performance for the Queen of Belgium. Usually, a woman her age would be considered too old for a ballerina; most dancers stopped performing in their forties. But her power and magic did not diminish with age, and she had continued to dance. The Queen and the audience looked forward to her appearance. However, a few days before the performance, the theater manager received the shocking news that Pavlova had died suddenly in The Hague, on her way to Brussels.

The performance was not canceled, the theater was full, and even the Queen attended. When the time for Pavlova's solo came, the orchestra played the music for the Dying Swan, and a single, pure white ray of spotlight moved over the dark stage, following where Pavlova would have been moving as she danced. The Queen and the entire audience rose to their feet, and their eyes followed the white light until the end of the piece. An eerie tribute, fitting for the magical dancer.

Russian Pearl Embroidery

Natalya, the expert on Russian Pearl Embroidery, is highly valued in Madame Koska's atelier. It is a complicated, intricate form of embroidery, demanding perfection in the execution. The level of opulence achieved by this style is unmatched. The pearls themselves do not have to be very expensive, though beautifully rounded ones are preferred. But the combination of laying down gold couching thread, pearls, and sometimes other gems on brilliantly colored or thick black cloth, was fit for royalty, nobility, the church, and the fabulously wealthy.

Pearl embroidery is no longer in demand, but since some great craftspeople still make it, the art is not lost. Many elegant, vintage patterns still exist today and can be found searching on the Internet.

Who were the Russian mannequins in Paris of the 1920s?

Unlike today's models, the mannequins were not adolescents. Girls between the ages of fourteen to sixteen were not forced to diet into anorexia and stunt their development. They were not over six feet tall, made of skin and bone; they had real women's bodies. They possessed the obligatory tiny waist and long legs, but they were young ladies who looked charming and graceful in street clothes as well as on the runway.

In the 1920s, there were about a hundred young Russian women who worked as models in Paris. They were members of the exiled aristocracy, had no money, and needed employment—and the great couture houses were only too happy to take them. The young ladies had an excellent education and perfect manners and could converse with the clients with ease, not only because of their social habits and experience but also because French was the first language of the Russian nobility.

There was a strict hierarchy in the modeling profession. The models were divided into several categories: *Mannequins de cabine*, who were on the payroll for the couture house; *mannequins vedettes*, or "stars" who came for select shows, and *mannequins volantes*, or flying models, who were hired to travel with shows abroad. The last category, the *mannequins mondaines* (society models), were either particularly beautiful or had noble titles of the highest level. They did not appear in shows. They were given dresses to wear as they circulated in society, presenting the clothes to those attending balls, opera, and other social events.

The house of Chanel, for example, had two "star" mannequins. The first, Princess Mary Eristova, was born in Georgia, but her father, Prince Schervachidze, was a member of the *State Duma of Russia*, raising his daughter and her siblings in Saint Petersburg, where she became a lady-in-waiting for Empress Alexandra. When she arrived in Paris and was introduced to Coco Chanel, the couturier was impressed with her fragile, dark, exotic beauty that perfectly suited Chanel's style. Gali Bajenova, a tall blonde with a full figure, was the daughter of a famous general, Konstantin Nikolayevich Hagondokov. She came to Paris as a married woman and was also hired by Chanel to be a society model, showing the

Chanel dresses at many social events. Her pictures appeared regularly in popular fashion magazines.

Many noble families would have objected to their daughters doing any work at all—let alone showing themselves in public—but they had no choice. Many Russian immigrants left with absolutely nothing, and many of them had no marketable skills for anywhere other than Russia, where the fathers acted as officials and the mothers served at court. And modeling paid exceptionally well—a model could earn four times as much as a waitress or a shop girl. In addition, these young ladies had a love of fashion that helped them settle into the new life with a level of comfort. Many saw it as an adventure and enjoyed the trade and the social opportunities it brought.

I hope these bits of history help you enjoy the book. If you're interested in learning more, I encourage you to explore the Internet or the library.

To Lilah, Rachel, and Alan,
my combined inspiration for the unlikely mix of
literary crime and high fashion.

MADAME KOSKA & LE SPECTRE DE LA ROSE

One

"And here comes Miss Gretchen, vearing a dress inspired by Russian peasant designs but recreated with elegant fabrics instead of homespun cotton or vool. You vill notice that the overcoat, or *Zipun*, is made from chiffon, so it is sufficiently translucent to show the traditionally pearl-embroidered *Sarafan*, made of heavy velvet; you vill see the pearls more clearly as Miss Gretchen is taking off the *Zipun*. Note how the *Sarafan* flows from the shoulders to the floor, and since it is meant for evening vear, ve have dispensed with the blouse that is usually vorn under it. The pearls are embroidered vith silver rather than the traditional gold thread since it is more in tune with our theme tones. And here comes Miss Cornelia in a deep blue and grey gown. Notice the sapphires that surround the décolletage..."

Gretchen floated behind the cream-coloured curtain, the ephemeral outfit trailing after her, her gleaming amber hair shining softly in the sunlight. Miss Cornelia glided forward, her blond curls shimmering like a halo around her classically beautiful face. The third mannequin waited by the curtain, ready to be called, yet unseen. The fashion show was in full swing, going entirely according to Madame Koska's original plans.

Early on she had decided to call it *Mistral*, after the north wind that blew grey and lavender clouds over stormy skies. Everything was designed in blue, purple, lavender and grey. Morning and afternoon outfits, elegantly tailored, and evening dresses flowing over the body like water appeared one after the other, the fabrics swishing seductively. They were beaded with extravagance; everyone could recognise the Russian opulence superimposed over the Parisian elegance.

Madame Koska noted with deep satisfaction that the room was packed. The light and airy hall sparkled with flower arrangements of blue irises, white calla lilies, and small lavender and purple hothouse anemones that reflected the fabric tones. The scent of expensive perfumes, flowers, and tobacco permeated the warm atmosphere. The afternoon sun streamed diagonally through the enormous windows, illuminating the room with shafts of golden light that showed the swirling smoke from many cigarettes. The guests sat around the well-appointed tables, covered with lacy white tablecloths and supporting heavy, real silver; they sipped their tea or coffee from thin, white china cups, hand-painted with tiny flowers and a thin rim of silver. The sumptuous food, catered by Madame Koska's great friend, Madame Anna Golitsyn, included many of her celebrated pastries, some Russian, some continental, and she added a touch of whimsy by decorating the petit fours in the colours of the *Mistral* collection and adding crystallised violets wherever possible.

Madame Koska had no doubt that the show would prove highly successful. Her air of confidence and complete control enhanced her elegance and charm that easily rivalled her mannequins' even if they were girls half her age. In her late forties, Madame Koska was a living proof of her own belief that a woman could be lovely at any age. With her tall, slim figure, perfectly displayed by the tailored grey silk suit, her almost line-free face with its fair skin, her chocolate-coloured eyes, and her dark brown, softly upswept hair, she would have looked ravishing in any of her creations.

As the show was reaching the end, Madame Koska glanced at the table where her close friends were sitting and smiled at the familiar faces. These were Madame Golitsyn and her niece Natalya Saltykov, who was Madame Koska's chief embroiderer and beader; Madame Golitsyn's brother Vasily and his girlfriend Wilma, who looked charming but out of place in her bold flapper outfit; Mr. Van der Hoven, who was Gretchen's father; Mr. Korolenko, with whom Madame Koska had, as she called it, an "understanding"; and she could not help being amused by the presence of Inspector Blount, an admirer of Natalya. He must have asked his friend Mr. Korolenko to bring him to the show since Madame Koska did not remember inviting him. To her surprise, she saw a stranger sitting by Madame Golitsyn. She must have come rather late, because Madame Koska did not notice her earlier. A slight, delicate woman no longer in her first youth, she was striking with her porcelain skin, dark eyes, and jet-black hair pulled back in a tight, glossy high chignon. Madame Koska found her vaguely familiar, but could not place her and did not have time to think about it since many people were approaching her. Some wanted to congratulate her on the lovely show, others to request an appointment with the intent of buying one of the dresses or ordering another one, and several journalists asked the usual questions and took some photographs. She dealt graciously with everyone, and as the room emptied, approached her friends who remained sitting at their table, waiting for her.

Madame Golitsyn handed her a well-deserved cup of tea, and everyone began talking all at once, shaking her hand, or hugging her. Only Natalya sat quietly, smiling with such deep and sincere happiness that it touched Madame Koska's heart. *Mistral* was Natalya's first opportunity to show her magnificent work to a large buying public, and since the occasion was so successful, her future in the industry was assured. It represented a milestone for the young woman who had bravely decided to forget her glorious past in prerevolutionary Russia and adjust, albeit with difficulty, to the life of a working woman.

"The last show for your little Gretchen, at least for a vhile," Madame Koska said to Mr. Van der Hoven.

"Yes, soon she will go off to the university," said Mr. Van der Hoven proudly. "But she tells me she will return to the world of fashion when she gets her degree."

"I vill be happy to have her," said Madame Koska. "But of course, she vill no longer be a mannequin. She can be a vonderful vendeuse, so talented and tactful."

"I can't see her buried in academia," said Wilma. "She is just too beautiful for such a life."

"But too intelligent not to earn a degree," said Mr. Korolenko. "I am glad you are sending her to the university, Mr. Van der Hoven." Everyone nodded in agreement.

"A university-educated voman vith good business sense and good style is a treasure," said Madame Koska.

Mr. Van der Hoven smiled at her gratefully.

"Miss Saltykov, three vomen said they vanted to buy Russian embroidery," said Madame Koska, smiling at Natalya. "And Annushka, *dorogaya*, everyone raved about your food, as alvays." Madame Golitsyn smiled at her friend.

"Thank you, my dear; I am so happy about it. But we must not forget our guest," said Madame Golitsyn. "I would like you to meet my old friend, Madame Galina Danilova."

Madame Koska laughed. "I thought I knew you, Madame Danilova. I have attended so many of your performances, but somehow I did not recognise you."

"That is natural," said Madame Danilova. "We look quite different on stage. The ballet gives us a certain magic that disappears when we are seen in broad daylight."

"I am so pleased to meet you," said Madame Koska. "I truly admire your dancing, and your entire group, really, is such a delight."

"I must tell it to my husband," said Madame Danilova, smiling. "He will be overjoyed to hear it, particularly since he sent me as an emissary. He would have come himself, but sitting still for hours at a fashion show is not a favourite thing with him, I am afraid. He is too restless."

"An emissary? For vhat reason?" asked Madame Koska, smiling.

"He is determined that you design the costumes for a new and innovative ballet, which we are going to premiere in London in the autumn," said Madame Danilova.

Madame Koska was taken aback, so much so that she forgot her manners and stared at the prima ballerina. "But…I have never designed for the ballet! Besides, you have your famous house designer!"

"Yes, but Monsieur Bex is on business in the United States for at least a year, so he is not available for the London show. My husband feels it would be nice to have a fresh approach." Madame Danilova sipped her coffee and smiled as if the matter was settled.

Madame Koska knew she should not undertake the assignment. It was not a good idea on any level. Sasha Danilov, the famous impresario of the *Ballet Baikal*, had the reputation of being difficult, demanding, aggressive, and unreasonable. Not a personality Madame Koska would wish to work with. He was also known for his creativity, culture, and hypnotic charm that made everyone submit to his iron will. He often experienced terrible money difficulties due to his bad business practices. But then again, he always managed to get out of trouble in the end, and he was basically honest. His ballets were pure enchantment, and Madame Koska loved the art, finding herself transported by it to a faraway fantasy land. But no, no, no! She will adamantly refuse to do it. It spelled nothing but trouble… Money and time would be terribly wasted; impossible, quite impossible… And yet, such a challenge, creating costumes that would move, sway, dance, and become virtually alive… No! It would be madness, pure madness! Out of the question, and that's it! She will adamantly refuse!

"Very vell, Madame Danilova," said Madame Koska. "Vhy don't you come to my atelier tomorrow, so ve can discuss it and see vhat ve can do..." and she pulled her card out of her bag and handed it to the ballerina.

Workers began to move about the empty hall, throwing glances of disapproval at their table, the last one to be occupied. They wished to get on with their work.

"Time for all my dear guests to go home and rest," said Madame Koska. "Madame Golitsyn and I vill stay to supervise the dismantling of the show and of the catering equipment, but the rest of you must leave... they are trying to finish off."

"It has been such a great pleasure to be together again," said Vasily. "Do you remember how we enjoyed our Christmas dinner at the Petrograd Room? I do wish we could do it again sooner than next Christmas."

"Yes, what a lovely traditional dinner it was, darlings," said Wilma. "Is there any other holiday soon? A real Russian one?"

"As a matter of fact, there is," said Mr. Korolenko. "Easter is almost upon us."

"Indeed!" said Madame Golitsyn. "Let us have a wonderful traditional Easter dinner at the Petrograd Room. I'll make reservations tomorrow. Mr. Van der Hoven, you must bring Gretchen to this celebration. You will both enjoy it."

"We would love to," said Mr. Van der Hoven. "Thank you!"

"Madame Danilova, would you come and bring your husband?" said Madame Koska.

"I am sure he would be more than happy," said Madame Danilova. "And so would I!"

"So it's arranged, but we really must leave," said Mr. Korolenko. "Madame Danilova, don't forget to tell Sasha I will visit him while he is in London. It's been years..."

"Is there anyone you don't know personally?" asked Madame Koska, laughing.

"Not if they are from Saint Petersburg or Moscow," said Mr. Korolenko. "Such a small society; we all know each other."

"Miss Saltykov, may I take you home, since your aunt is staying here?" asked Inspector Blount who never missed an opportunity to spend time with Natalya.

"Yes, thank you, Inspector," said Natalya, "unless Madame Koska will allow me to stay and help packing."

"Packing, in this lovely dress, my dear?" said Madame Koska. "No, no. Go and rest. We have enough people here who are ready to do the packing. I'll see you tomorrow at the atelier."

Looking after Natalya, Madame Golitsyn smiled. "Yes, she would be willing to get herself dirty packing and carrying in the pretty dress she worked so hard on. She is so happy with you. I believe her adjustment is complete. She no longer thinks about her past as Countess Natalya Saltykov at the Tsar's court…she is quite happy in her new role as a middle-class designer and craftswoman. Do you remember her old friend, Lady Victoria?"

"Yes, of course. She is coming to the atelier soon for summer clothes."

"Natalya visits her sometimes, and enjoys the evenings, but when I asked her about any eligible young men of the upper classes who may take an interest in her, she made it very clear that she would not welcome such an occurrence. She is proud of her position at what she calls The Best Atelier in the World."

Madame Koska was touched. "In the future, when I begin to contemplate retirement, I will offer her a position of a junior partner. I know she is not any good with business, but we both know who is… I can see Gretchen, as the business partner, and Natalya, as the designing partner, doing a very good job running the atelier when I am gone."

"Don't rush into it," said Madame Golitsyn, smiling. "We want to have you run this wonderful atelier for many years to come."

"Far future, then," said Madame Koska, laughing. "Tell me, Annushka, did Natalya design this dress, or make it from a pattern?"

"She designed it," said Madame Golitsyn. "She always does."

"I think I am going to ask her to design some dresses for me," said Madame Koska. "She is very good; this dress was truly beautiful. And so was the suit I saw her wearing at the Christmas dinner. But I'd like her to gain experience designing for others. I'll do it very slowly so as not to frighten her."

"Wonderful," said Madame Golitsyn.

At four o'clock the next day Madame Danilova arrived at the atelier, with the punctuality of a woman used to rigorous schedules. Madame Koska escorted her to the office, ordered tea, and closed the door. Madame Danilova looked around her with pleasure. "Such a nice office," she said. "It must be comfortable to do business here. My husband's business activities are done on tiny little bits of paper, he never sits at a desk, and the details are in his head instead of in documents."

Madame Koska laughed. "And yet he is such a successful impresario, Madame Danilova, famous all over Europe, Russia, and the United States. You must lead an exciting life vith him."

"I suppose," said Madame Danilova. "But it can be exhausting. We hardly stay anywhere for more than a season; it's a nomadic life. We don't even own a home, Madame Koska. We live in hotels. Luxurious and comfortable hotels, I must admit, but I miss having a home, preferably right here in London. As you know, I am English, despite my assumed stage name, so I miss a permanent place here, not to mention that I am not getting any younger."

"Ah, no, you are young and beautiful, and you dance like an angel," said Madame Koska.

"Thank you, my dear," said Madame Danilova. "I am so glad I appear that way. And I am doubly happy because I will be dancing the ballet you are going to design your lovely clothes for."

"You are the prima ballerina for all of the ballets, I think?" said Madame Koska, surprised.

"Not anymore. Certain leading parts go to the ingénues; it's only natural," said Madame Danilova. "I am not sad about it; such is the way of the world. For example, in the production we are going to discuss, I am dancing the long ballet. However, there are two short ballets that will be presented first. I will not be in either of them." She smiled, seemingly without resentment.

"I see," said Madame Koska, wondering if the prima ballerina was really as calm about it as she seemed. The career of a ballerina was so short...certainly all dancers were aware of it from the start, but facing the end, so quickly, must be harsh. Madame Danilova seemed to be only in her early forties. "So who vill be dancing these parts?" she asked.

"The same girl who is performing in *Le Spectre de la Rose* which is part of our program this season. Usually we do our own, new choreographies. But this time, we received permission from the owners to perform *Le Spectre de la Rose* in London. Everyone loves this piece! She is French and just out of the ballet academy. She is very good, but I am a bit worried about it."

"Vhy is that?"

"Because she is only good, not great. It may take years to achieve greatness. The male part, the Spectre, is danced by our star, Victor Parizhsky. Calling Victor a great performer is an understatement. His performance is so extraordinary, that it is considered by some to be supernatural...the results of their dancing together are uneven. When you dance a *pas de deux*, it can lead to failure if one of the couple is always trying to catch up." She sighed.

"Did you say anything to your husband?" asked Madame Koska.

"Yes. I suggested that he might select another male dancer for the piece, and he agreed at first, but when he told Victor, there was a scene of such magnitude, such drama, that Sasha backed off. He can't refuse Victor anything, particularly if he cries. And believe me, Victor sobbed."

"I heard that Monsieur Parizhsky is living vith you, like an adopted son," said Madame Koska. "You must both love him very much."

Madame Danilova looked at her as if she thought Madame Koska was trying to mock or insult her, her eyes full of rage. Suddenly she must have realised that Madame Koska was saying exactly what she thought with complete innocence. She shrugged and relaxed. "No, Madame Koska. I see that you don't know the real situation. About ten years ago Sasha asked me to marry him because he wanted to hush up the scandals that were circulating about him and some boys who danced at the *Ballet Baikal*. He and Victor are lovers. The arrangement of marriage and living together worked for everyone, since I did not want to have a personal life and a real husband; it would have interfered with my career."

Madame Koska nodded. "Yes, I see. Indeed, people can be so ridiculous in their criticism of any lifestyle that is not exactly like their own. I think that your arrangement vas a very good idea."

Madame Danilova smiled. "I am glad you understand; it is such a pleasure to talk to a woman of the world, Madame Koska."

Madame Koska shrugged. "It's important to keep an open mind about all matters," she said. "And if the three of you are finding the arrangement vorkable, vhy not?"

"Exactly. We get along very well. Victor is a quiet, shy creature when away from the stage, and does not connect easily with most people. But he trusts me, and I believe even likes me very much. I certainly like him, poor soul."

"Poor soul? The most famous dancer in the vorld?" asked Madame Koska, surprised.

"He suffers from bouts of depression, and no wonder. The young male dancers live a harsh life," said Madame Danilova. "From an early age, almost as children, they realise that they must accept the advances of the older, rich patrons of the ballet, or of the managers and impresarios. This form of prostitution is customary and they would never get ahead otherwise; the competition is fierce. They are so obsessed with the ballet that they do not care about sacrificing themselves, but it takes its toll as they are passed from hand to hand. Victor was the lover of an influential nobleman, a great patron of the ballet, who got tired of him. The nobleman simply wrote a note to Sasha, explaining that he knew a boy, a fantastic dancer and quite attractive, whom he thought Sasha should meet. This was the reward he gave the boy—introduction to the great impresario. Sasha sent a note to summon the boy, fell in love at first sight, hired him without even checking his performance, and had him spend the night."

"It is rather harsh, I must admit," said Madame Koska. "I vonder vhat vould have happened if Victor did not justify his reputation as a great dancer."

"Nothing terrible, Sasha is too kind to just tell him to leave. He would have Victor join the corps de ballet, or perhaps introduce him to another gentleman...who knows; Sasha always finds a way. Luckily, Victor turned out to be the best dancer Sasha had ever met, and in addition, Sasha truly loves Victor, and treats him well; it's not always like that, though." She sighed. "But we must discuss the costumes! The ballet we are working on is highly innovative. You will not believe it, but we will not dance *en pointe*! We will be barefoot."

"Really? How interesting," said Madame Koska. "Vhat is the name of the ballet?"

"*The Flight of Icarus*. It is a Greek myth about a boy who flew into the sun and fell to earth. My husband and the choreographer feel they can show off Victor's ability to soar into the air as he does the *grand jeté* and other such aerial moves. His ability to stay in the air is indeed a little frightening, even though I know how he does it."

"Can you tell me?" asked Madame Koska, who had heard all the superstitious nonsense that was regularly told about Victor Parizhsky. While she did not believe it, she could not understand his leaps either.

Madame Danilova laughed. "It's not a secret—he simply has extremely strong toes. When he lands, he does not fall on the ball of the foot, like other male dancers, but lands on his toes, and then very slowly lowers the foot. These extra seconds somehow create the illusion of flight, particularly with the right lighting. In *Le Spectre de la Rose*, there is even a mechanical contraption to help the illusion when the Spectre jumps out of the window before the end of the piece. I'll show it to you when you come to the theatre. It's quite effective—you would imagine Victor is soaring into the night sky."

"How fascinating," said Madame Koska. "Yes, he vill do vell as Icarus. So the costumes should be Greek."

"Yes, but we would like some fantasy. It does not have to be accurately Greek, just the spirit of the time and place; it is important to create a sense of flight, and then express the closeness to the sun when the wings begin to melt. The colours would be significant, I imagine."

"Yes, ve must move from cool colours as he and his father Daedalus begin the flight, to very hot colours when Icarus comes close to the sun, and then back to cool, or even dark colours as he falls to his death and his father mourns him," said Madame Koska, pulling a drawing pad towards her. "I imagine the lighting can be helpful, too, if the fabric's colour is more or less neutral."

"So you know the story," said Madame Danilova with approval.

"Oh, yes, I love mythology," said Madame Koska. "It vill be an adventure to design for such a project."

"You must come to a rehearsal, and then discuss the terms with Sasha," said Madame Danilova. "Would you be able to come tomorrow morning?"

There was no going back, but Madame Koska had already forgotten her misgivings anyway, and glorious costumes were swirling in her mind. How does one create wings that are large enough to take a muscular young man to the sky, but not so heavy as to drag him down as Victor Parizhsky performs his legendary leaps?

Two

Madame Koska felt she had stepped into another world. The ballet was like nothing she had ever seen. She was not even sure she could define it as ballet. The dancers, all female, worked on a bare stage with no scenery, but the wildness of the jerky movements suggested a bacchanal. However, it was different from the bacchanals she was used to seeing in several operas, and certainly not as tame. The music consisted of a cacophony of percussion and wind instruments. Every so often a burst of string instruments erupted from the orchestra, seemingly out of place. The dancers wore the usual rehearsal clothes and no shoes, as Madame Danilova had explained, so they were a rather plain group, but as Madame Koska was watching, the images began to shift in front of her inner eye—she was always ready to design. She envisioned the dancers in Greek-influenced tunics, ephemeral white on blue. There was no magical lighting, no shadow at all under the bright lights that illuminated the stage, and yet the dancers succeeded in creating an aura of mystery and timelessness.

Suddenly, a male figure flew into the scene. The sheer height of the leap was startling, but the sensation of slow hovering, of real flight, was disconcerting. It was simply impossible—no one could stay up in the air like that—but one could not deny it as it happened in front of one's eyes. Madame Koska held her breath as he smoothly merged with the wild female group, swaying and undulating. The musical instruments screamed, and the segment of ballet came to an end. Madame Koska breathed again.

She was still slightly dazed as she watched the dancers disappear behind the stage, and was startled when she saw a person approaching her. He was a strongly built man of middle height, wrapped in a large overcoat with a fur collar. Madame Koska estimated him at about fifty years old. He had a large face, a generous, full mouth with thick lips, and a strange white streak divided his black hair. He could have been thought unprepossessing or even downright ugly, but his brown eyes were so full of intelligence and enthusiasm, there was so much life and power in his personality, that somehow, he appeared to be quite attractive in a strange, almost savage way.

"Madame Koska, I am delighted you have consented to design the costumes," he said as he bowed gallantly over her hand. "We must speak French...it is our common language when my wife joins us. I don't speak very good English, I am afraid, and she does not speak Russian." At this time Madame Koska could speak Russian reasonably well, after the extensive studies with Mr. Korolenko, but nevertheless she was relieved. With so much work to concentrate on, she did not need to worry about making language mistakes.

"I am most pleased to meet you, Monsieur Danilov," she said. "I have taken on the job despite serious misgivings—simply because I could not resist the challenge and the pleasure. I adore the ballet."

The impresario laughed heartily. "I am so glad I did not have to spend days convincing you, Madame Koska. I would have persuaded you at last, but it would have taken so much time...much better like this." Madame Koska believed him. There was no doubt this man always got what he wanted.

"We must go somewhere and discuss terms," said the impresario. "Have you had breakfast? Let's go to a café and have some. Here comes Galina. Let's go." So Madame Danilova was telling the truth, thought Madame Koska. The great man did not bother keeping an office.

At the café, over a continental breakfast, M. Danilov explained that they were having two separate productions in London. They were performing traditional pieces over the next two months in London, *The Spectre de la Rose* and *Giselle*, while rehearsing for the controversial and modern *The Flight of Icarus*, and two other short pieces he was considering, to be presented in the fall. After that, M. Danilov was making arrangements in the United States for a tour that would last a year.

"Vhat an exciting life," said Madame Koska. "It must take a tremendous amount of energy to keep everything in order."

"I love it," said M. Danilov with childlike simplicity. "I could never live a normal life. Of course, there are always troubles. Money, mostly. There is never enough money, ever. We make so much, but it is swallowed by the productions and admittedly, by the lifestyle. There is always the need to treat, to entertain, to buy gifts, to throw parties; it never ends."

"This is inevitable," said Madame Danilova. "Promoting is everything; we depend on it."

"And I am sure you have some trouble keeping so many personalities in order, some of them sensitive and proud, others jealous and angry," said Madame Koska.

"Oh, yes," said the impresario. "Every single one of them thinks he or she is the most important personage. They are all divas. And among them are people who would stab others in the back for a better part, or a favour. But I enjoy these challenges, and somehow everything turns out all right in the end. I am not sure why."

"I am no diva," said Madame Danilova, smiling.

"You, a diva?" said M. Danilov in mock horror. "The mere thought! No one would suspect!" They all laughed.

"So, I have a couple of months for the creation of the costumes. Very vell, ve must start immediately," said Madame Koska. "There is not a moment to lose."

"I am delighted by your efficiency," said M. Danilov. "The dancers will be at your disposal. They rehearse in the morning, and have performances in the evening, but we do not have many matinees; they can come to your atelier almost any day between two and six."

"Excellent," said Madame Koska. "And now, as for the terms…"

"Yes, indeed. Let me see, is there a clean napkin here…" he turned to the empty table behind him and pulled a clean linen napkin from under the silver that was arranged over it. The silver fell to the floor, and a waiter quickly came to pick it up. "Ah, waiter, bring me a pencil," said the impresario, searching in his pockets. "No, don't bother. I have found my pen." Under Madame Koska's astonished eyes, he wrote "Costumes" on the napkin, and they launched into a discussion regarding payments, schedules of deliveries, and such like, all of which he scribbled in detail on the napkin.

"Do you always do your business so informally?" asked Madame Koska, amused.

"This is more formal than scribbling on his shirt cuffs," said Madame Danilova, laughing. "He often does that, and then if the shirt is sent to the laundry by mistake, what a disaster! The napkin won't get lost, you see? He'll keep it in his pocket until he gets back to his staff… And don't worry. Somebody will send you everything written neatly on paper for your signatures."

Madame Koska laughed. "That is good since I vould not like to sign a napkin!"

"I imagine you are highly organised, Madame Koska. Everything in its place, as they say?"

"She is, Sasha. Her office is delightfully arranged in perfect order," said Madame Danilova.

"I am afraid so," said Madame Koska. "Such pedantry must seem boring to you, but it's a habit with me, and it saves me from much trouble." For a moment she thought about the horrible mess of papers she had to sort out when her husband embezzled his own atelier and disappeared. But she forced herself to come back to the present and smiled. She did not know if M. Danilov was aware of her past, and she did not want to discuss it.

The meeting ended by deciding that Victor Parizhsky and Galina Danilova, the two principals of *The Flight of Icarus*, would visit the atelier for measurements in two days. In the meantime, Madame Koska would have time to make a few preliminary sketches to show them.

As soon as Madame Koska returned to the atelier, Gretchen, who was acting as vendeuse as usual until her university course was to start, handed her the telephone. It was Mr. Korolenko.

"Would you like to go and see the current ballet?" he asked. "They are dancing two delightful pieces, *Le Spectre de la Rose* and *Giselle*."

"Yes, I vould love to go," said Madame Koska. "It vill be a good idea to get used to the vay they dance. I have never seen *Giselle*."

"Have you seen *Le Spectre*?" asked Mr. Korolenko.

"Yes, years ago in Paris. I saw it with the original dancer. He was incredibly good, and it would be interesting to compare his performance with that of Victor Parizhsky."

"I can have tickets for tomorrow night, if you like, or even tonight," said Mr. Korolenko.

"Let me guess," said Madame Koska, laughing. "Even though the performance may be sold out, you have some influence with M. Danilov. So let's go tonight!"

"Of course I have influence with Sasha... Let me find out what time the show begins and I'll let you know."

"Thank you," said Madame Koska, and hung up.

Neither of them mentioned an important issue. Some months ago, they were both involved in a grand theft of jewelry which put both their lives in danger. When the crime was solved, mostly by Madame Koska, Mr. Korolenko made his feelings for her known, and while Madame Koska had always thought she could never love again, she found herself falling for the sophisticated, handsome, brilliant man who had that touch of mystery and intrigue which made him irresistible. But she was not in a rush. She had explained that yes, she would welcome him into her life, but for the near future, she simply had to concentrate on creating the *Mistral* fashion show and could not start a new relationship. Mr. Korolenko was perfectly agreeable to the "understanding" between them, and refrained from pressing her, or even mentioning the situation.

They saw each other often. Mr. Korolenko was a linguist and a professor of languages, among other pursuits. Madame Koska, despite her convincing Russian accent, did not speak Russian. She was an Englishwoman who had married an upper-class Russian man in Paris, and since he was the owner of a successful fashion atelier, frequented by many noble Russian émigrés, he thought it advisable that his wife and business partner would also appear to be of the Russian upper classes. She quickly learned to adopt a fake Russian accent which she could use equally well in English and in French. When she moved to London, some years after the terrible scandal caused by her missing husband, she realised the sham could not go on unless she learned Russian. In Paris, her clients, even the Russian ones, spoke French. In London, they tended to speak Russian among themselves and English with the natives. Mr. Korolenko was introduced to her by Madame Golitsyn.

Madame Koska had sometimes wondered how Mr. Korolenko would approach this uncomfortable little dilemma when the *Mistral* show was over. With her hand still hovering over the phone, she realised how discreetly he had already started to change the rules of the game. The ballet would be the first time they would attend any performance, or even a restaurant, without the company of others. Yes, it would be a most elegant way to start the new relationship and quite typical of Mr. Korolenko's way of handling delicate situations. She smiled at Gretchen, took off her coat, and went to her office. There she sat down at her desk, pulled out a long cigarette holder from her purse, put a cigarette in it and lighted it, deep in thought. Was she truly ready for the new phase in her life? She placed the cigarette holder on an ashtray, removed her rings and took off her white gloves, then put her rings back on her hands. She thought of her husband and knew that once and for all, he was gone forever, not only from her life, but from her thoughts and feelings. Was it the right time? Yes, she decided. It's time. I am ready.

Three

The theatre seemed different at night. It was rather stark during her morning visit, but quite festive and beautifully lit at night. The shafts of cigarette smoke were visible under the golden lights, their odor mixing with the different perfumes everyone wore. The air was warm and slightly thick but not oppressive, perhaps a little intoxicating. Madame Koska and Mr. Korolenko were escorted to their excellent seats at the seventh row centre in the Stalls, were handed the programme, and sat down on the plush red chairs.

"This is interesting," said Madame Koska. "Dmitry, look at the picture of M. Parizhsky on the cover. They have the original costume—the one I saw in Paris."

Using Mr. Korolenko's Christian name in public was another first. Until this time, they used first names only in private. But it was time for her to show him she could adjust to the new situation. Madame Koska noticed a fleeting smile on his face, but he said nothing about it. Instead, he asked, "How can you tell it's the same one?"

"Vell...costumes are my trade. I vould recognise these roses, particularly the petals, anywhere. Do you know, they used to sew the original dancer into the costume for every performance? It fitted perfectly—such beautiful vork. I vonder if they do it with M. Parizhsky."

The theatre started to darken; quiet fell on the chattering crowd. The curtain rose on the stage of *Le Spectre de la Rose*. Based on a poem by Théophile Gautier, describing the spirit of the special rose a young girl is wearing to a ball, and the music of Carl Maria von Weber's *Invitation to the Dance*, it had little story but plenty of opportunity to show technique and style. The stage represented the girl's simple bedroom, done entirely in blue and white, with one alcove draped with hangings made of semi-transparent tulle. A few chairs, and a piece of embroidery that had not been put away before the girl had left was placed on a table. The girl danced into her room, graceful, young, and happy after the ball, which she obviously had enjoyed very much. She carried a pink rose. Was it her first ball? Most likely. Did someone special give her the rose? We would never know. The girl sank gracefully into a chair, her eyes closed, and dreaming, lost the rose which fell to the floor. At this moment, all those who had seen the ballet before tensed up, ready for the well-known surprise that never failed to startle you anyway—the Spectre's first *grand jeté* into the room through one of the windows. The entire audience gasped. No dancer had ever been able to rise in the air, remain motionless, and then slowly descend, like Victor Parizhsky. It was impossible, improbable. He hovered like a bird, then landed softly next to the sleeping girl. He whirled around the room and then around the girl, finally drawing her to her feet, still asleep, to dance with him.

While the girl was wearing a chaste, simple, white dress and a little bonnet, the Spectre's costume was calculated to startle the audience. It was multi-coloured—pink, rose, red, and green—comprised of a tunic that was covered with silk petals and some roses. High on his arms he wore two armbands that were also covered with the same materials, and also flowers in his cap. This was neither a masculine nor a feminine costume--it was unique, magical, and disturbing. The genderless spirit moved his arms softly in a style that male dancers did not employ. It was not that he embodied a bisexual being—there was no sexuality in it at all—it was entirely spiritual, as if the dancer were an angel, a being of another world, neither male nor female. As he danced, many silk petals and a few silk roses fell from the costume, floated gently down, and landed on the floor.

Madame Koska smiled. She remembered the story that was told about the original dancer's valet—he used to collect the petals and sell them to admirers, earning a good income out of this little side business. She wondered if Victor Parizhsky knew about it.

The spirit bent over the girl, and drew her, still sleeping, into a dance. The dance signified love in its purest and most spiritual form, bringing the wonderful music to life. At the end of the dance, the Spectre settled the girl back in her chair and kissed her very gently. He then turned, and to the joy of the audience, performed the most celebrated *grand jeté* as he flew out of the window into the night. Madame Koska knew the technique of it. She was told about the five running steps from the middle of the stage, and then the leap at the sixth step from a low baseboard. She knew that behind the set, four men would catch Victor Parizhsky in the air, in such a way that no one could see the landing—or even the descent from the height of the leap. She knew that the conductor would enhance the illusion by holding the last chord for a longer time than usual, suggesting that out there, the Spectre was still flying. Knowing did not matter at all; when one looked at Victor Parizhsky, one believed that he could fly, that a miracle had happened.

Madame Koska, who had held her breath since before the final *grand jeté*, relaxed. The thought crossed her mind that Madame Danilova was right. The young French ballerina was certainly good, but not great, and her dancing, while quite enjoyable, did not inspire. Victor Parizhsky dominated the piece. But the next performance was *Giselle*, and Madame Danilova in the title role was not shadowed by Victor Parizhsky. They were perfectly matched, and the sad story unfolded like a glittering dream. As always, Ballet Baikal delivered a magnificent performance.

Slightly dazed, as she always felt after a great ballet or a truly superior concert, Madame Koska left with Mr. Korolenko, and they stepped into the clear, chilly spring evening. It was only a step to a café they both knew, and they decided to go in for a light supper.

"A magnificent performance," said Mr. Korolenko. "Sasha may look and act like a barbarian, but he expresses all his inner beauty through the ballet."

"Vhat did you think of Madame Danilova's performance?" asked Madame Koska. "I thought she vas peerless. I don't understand vhy some of the parts are going to the younger girls. The French ballerina is not up to dancing with Victor Parizhsky."

"I don't understand it either," said Mr. Korolenko. "Perhaps there is a reason we don't know..." He seemed thoughtful. After a few minutes of silence, he said "Vera, the Mistral show is over..."

"So it is, Dmitry," said Madame Koska. "And it vas a bigger success than I had the right to expect. Everything should go very smoothly from now on at the atelier."

"Indeed," said Mr. Korolenko. "You may find some time to relax..."

"I intend to," said Madame Koska. She looked at the handsome face across the table, the warm brown eyes smiling at her, and smiled back. Yes, she thought. It's high time to make a change, to have a private life as well as a rewarding career. She finished her coffee, put her gloves on, and rearranged her rings on top of them. Mr. Korolenko turned to summon the waiter.

Since the atelier was not very far from the restaurant, they decided to walk. They did not talk very much; it did not seem necessary to either of them. When they reached the atelier, Madame Koska asked, "Would you like to come in for a drink, Dmitry?"

"Yes, I would like that very much," said Mr. Korolenko.

Madame Koska pulled the key out of her bag and offered it to him. Mr. Korolenko took the key, raised her hand to his lips, and opened the door.

When Madame Danilova and Victor Parizhsky entered the atelier, Madame Koska was surprised to see that a young lady came with them. She welcomed them cordially and led them to her office. Gretchen already knew she must order coffee and tea for the visitors.

"Madame Koska, may I introduce Mademoiselle Solange Forestier?" said Madame Danilova. Madame Koska recognised the dancer, who had been Victor's partner in *Le Spectre de la Rose*. "I am delighted to meet you, Mademoiselle Forestier. I have seen you dance and enjoyed your performance very much." The young woman smiled, shook Madame Koska's hand, and thanked her.

"We brought Mademoiselle Forestier with us, Madame Koska, since she is my understudy for *Icarus*," said Madame Danilova. "She must be measured for the same costume as myself."

"Of course," said Madame Koska, hiding her surprise. This new girl would be the understudy? Why not one of the experienced ballerinas who had been with the Ballet Baikal for years? A special costume? Normally the understudy would wear the costume that was prepared for the star, fitted as well as possible at the last moment. An extra costume that may never be used was an expensive luxury—and the two women were pretty much the same size, anyway. Strange...thought Madame Koska.

"And would you kindly meet Monsieur Parizhsky, our premier dancer?" Madame Koska shook the young man's hand. "I vas thrilled by your interpretation of *Le Spectre*, M. Parizhsky," she said, and catching herself in time, as she realised how much stronger her language was in praising Victor than Solange, continued, "Your *pas de deux* was inspirational. You both have created a whole new approach to this delightful piece." The young woman laughed good-naturally and said, "It will be years before I can even begin to hope to match M. Parizhsky's performance, if ever, Madame Koska. He is carrying me along in his performance, and I am grateful to him!" Victor shook his head and said, "No, no…" feebly dismissing the statement. The strong personality, fire, and passion—so obvious on stage—were not there at all. It was as if a light that had burned brightly inside the dancer while he was on stage was turned off, leaving an empty shell behind. Victor Parizhsky's dark eyes had no brilliance, his smile was vacuous, and he said very little. Madame Koska had an uncomfortable feeling that he was not fully there, that his mind wandered into another place and time.

One of the seamstresses entered with the tea tray, and Madame Koska handed cups all around. "Vould you like me to show you the sketches vhile ve are having our tea?" asked Madame Koska.

"Yes, I can't wait to see them," said Madame Danilova, smiling brightly. Madame Koska noted that the ballerina looked tired, almost haggard. Was she exhausted by the morning's exercises, on top of the nightly show? Quite possibly. Victor also looked tired, very tired. Mademoiselle Forestier seemed bright and cheery; she was the only one of the dancers to take a piece of cake with her tea. Victor hesitated, but when he saw that Madame Danilova did not take food, he refused it too.

Madame Koska brought out a few sketches. The woman's costume was made for a high priestess. A full, loose, flowing tunic reached just over the knees. It was all white. A gold belt was tied high, empire style, and then crossed between the breasts and over the neck. A short, sleeveless blue vest was worn above it, drawn to show it was made of a shiny material. The high priestess was barefoot, with a gold anklet on each leg, and a gold band circled her loose, long black hair.

Icarus's costume was shown in three different drawings. The first, which was marked "Neutral colour" was a short tunic worn over a pair of tights and simply belted. The colour was a plain beige-ecru. The second, marked "Blue light, cool" showed the costume as it would be lit right after the wings were attached by Icarus's father, Daedalus. It was azure blue, cool and pleasant. The wings were large and impressive. The third was marked "Near the sun, warm" and was shown in a combination of orange and red.

"How lovely," said Solange. "Though if I ever have to dance it, and of course I hope I will never have to, my dear Madame Danilova, would it look nice with my blonde hair?"

"Oh, yes," said Madame Koska. "Vhite and blue, with gold touches? Vonderful for a blonde."

Victor was looking at the Icarus sketch. He said nothing, but looked at Madame Danilova for guidance.

"This is magnificent," said Madame Danilova. "Both my costume and Victor's costumes are wonderful. How are you going to construct the wings?" Victor seemed relieved and lost interest.

"The ving's structure vill be made as a tube. Ve vill insert flexible vire into the tube, and so ve vill be able to shape it to any form ve need. Then ve vill cover it vith tulle and sew feathers onto it. They vill be extremely light, so ve vill experiment vith several sizes, to see vhat M. Parizhsky is comfortable vith."

Victor, hearing his name, looked at Madame Danilova to see if anything was needed. She smiled at him reassuringly and he relaxed. "This is a magnificent design, Madame Koska," said the ballerina.

After the tea, Madame Koska placed each of the dancers in a fitting room, where a seamstress was waiting to measure them. Victor, with whom she entered the room, did not bother to go behind the screen. Entirely oblivious to the presence of the seamstress and Madame Koska, he started to take off his clothes in the middle of the room, throwing them carelessly on a chair. Madame Koska was somewhat startled until she saw he wore a regular ballet leotard and tights under his clothes.

The dancer had a very unusual physique. His upper body was the torso of a strongly built, muscular young man, though not heavy. His lower body, however, looked almost as if it belonged to someone else. The muscles of his legs, both thighs and calves, were so heavily developed, that they were extremely large, completely out of proportion with his upper body. Madame Koska wondered why she could not see it when he was dancing. So much about this young man was baffling! Madame

Koska shrugged, gave a few last-minute instructions to the seamstress, made sure she took separate measurements of the forearm, upper arm, calf, and thigh, and went to see Madame Danilova.

"I hope you don't mind that we brought Solange," said the ballerina. "Seeing that it is the same costume, I thought it would be saving time for you."

"Not at all," said Madame Koska. "I vill be measuring the entire company soon. But is it really necessary to create an entire costume for her? I vas a little surprised."

Madame Danilova was quiet for a minute, looking a little thoughtful. "I will explain some other time," she said, raising her eyebrows significantly and pointedly looking at the busy seamstress who was on her knees, measuring Madame Danilova's length of calf.

"Of course," said Madame Koska, and tactfully changing the subject, reminded Madame Danilova about their promised Easter Sunday dinner at the Petrograd Room. Madame Danilova brightened and expressed her expectation of a very interesting and traditional experience.

"Miss Saltykov told me she vill have a little present for each of us," said Madame Koska. "She is preparing some very unusual Easter eggs."

"You mean the *pysanky* coloured eggs?" said Madame Danilova. "They are so lovely."

"No, better than that. She can do something I find almost miraculous—she can embroider the empty shell of an egg instead of colouring it; apparently, they do so in parts of the Ukraine," said Madame Koska, "but it's a rare thing. I have never heard of it."

"Embroider an egg?" asked Madame Danilova, astonished.

"Yes, there is a special technique for that, and specific tools. Miss Saltykov learned how to make them from a Ukrainian friend in Russia, and somehow Madame Golitsyn managed to buy the tools from an acquaintance recently. Miss Saltykov's skills are unmatched."

"Indeed. Madame Golitsyn and I have known each other for years, so I am familiar with her niece's work. Most impressive. Miss Saltykov gave me an embroidered set of handkerchiefs; I treasure them."

"Vell, I must go and see how Mademoiselle Forestier is faring," said Madame Koska. "After the session is over, I imagine you vill vant to rush back to the theatre to prepare for the evening performance, so I vill not detain you."

"No…" said Madame Danilova slowly, with some hesitation. "As a matter of fact, would it be possible for you to see me privately after the session? Just for a few minutes? I will send the others to the theatre. I won't take much of your time, but I really need to discuss something with you."

"Of course!" said Madame Koska brightly. "I'll make sure ve have some coffee and ve can talk! I'll tell Miss Van der Hoven that she should not allow anyone to disturb us."

❁

Sitting comfortably in the office, sipping her coffee, Madame Danilova still seemed fatigued and anxious. She put her cup down and said, "Madame Koska, what I am about to tell you is of the utmost secrecy."

"My dear Madame Danilova," said Madame Koska, "you can trust my discretion. I vill do anything to assist you."

"I would not burden you with this story if I did not think it was unfair for you to remain in the dark," said the ballerina, and was quiet again. For the first time Madame Koska noticed the ballerina had a few tiny white streaks in her jet-black hair, and some fine wrinkles on her fair skin. Madame Koska waited patiently for her guest to speak. Finally she said, "My husband would object to my telling you. I am doing it against his wishes."

"Are you sure you vish to tell me at all?" asked Madame Koska. "Vould it not cause trouble at home?"

"I must," said Madame Danilova. "The truth is, Madame Koska, I may be too sick to carry the burden of dancing the lead in *Icarus* in the autumn."

"Too sick?" asked Madame Koska, fearing the worst. "But you are dancing full-time these days...may I ask..."

"I am not dying, at least the doctors think I will live," said Madame Danilova gently. "I was diagnosed with tuberculosis. I have to go to Switzerland very soon, and stay some months in a specialized sanatorium."

"First of all, I am relieved that it is not vhat I thought it vas," said Madame Koska, not wishing to even mention the word "cancer."

"True. But it's entirely possible that my career is over...earlier than I thought; I believed I had a few more years. Two or three months away from practicing may destroy my skills. Still, the important thing is, of course, to listen to the doctors and try to heal as fast as I can."

"You alvays have the best attitude," said Madame Koska.

"I try," said the ballerina. "I always knew that in your forties, you have to stop dancing as a prima ballerina. Many of us move into teaching—and that is what I plan to do either way! But the issue of *Icarus* is not simple. Sasha thinks that if he cannot promote the ballet with me in it, it will greatly reduce the sales. I think Victor is the main attraction anyway, so it would not matter, but since Sasha is so worried, I promised him I will respect his wishes and tell no one. But I had to tell you, since it really looks so strange, creating the second costume. Sasha was adamant about it. He cares nothing about money, as you know...and he feels that he must cover all the possible situations."

"So vhat are you going to say?"

"Nothing. The rehearsals start at the end of June. Sasha hopes I will be well by then. If I can't come back at that time, he will have Solange do the rehearsals, still hoping I can come back any time until mid-August. He trusts I can rehearse the part quickly for the September show. Perhaps I can, particularly if he keeps sending me sheet music, transcripts of the ballet, and notes. At worst, if I can't come back at all, Solange will have to do it. But my name will be on all the promotions as if nothing happened, with her name as the understudy. The sales will be assured, and if at the last minute the world is told of the situation, they will most likely not cancel their tickets."

"I completely understand. To be honest, Madame Danilova, I agree vith your husband. Your name is essential on the programme."

"Thank you," said Madame Danilova. "It's all so difficult, and I am so glad I told you. It makes me feel so much better because I am really totally alone. Sasha would not listen to me, Victor thinks I am a tower of strength who must guide his every step, and the other ballerinas, including little Solange, just want to take my place…" She pulled a handkerchief from her bag and touched her eyes. That was all; she then raised her head and smiled bravely. But Madame Koska saw the lost, sad look in the ballerina's eyes, and her heart ached for Madame Danilova. Underneath the brave, practical façade, a very sad and lonely person was doing her best to handle a sea change, a complete transformation of her life. Madame Koska hoped her new friend would not break under the burden of loss, secrecy, illness, and isolation.

Four

"Annushka," said Madame Koska over the telephone, "I just had a telephone call from Madame Galina Danilova. She cannot come to our Easter dinner. The performances have been switched, for some reason; they show the *Spectre* and *Giselle* that night, and she dances *Giselle*, as you know. Remember? That was the one I saw with Dmitry. But her husband will join us, she said. I don't know if you would like to ask another person, or inform the Petrograd Room that we are one guest short."

"I'll let them know, Vera. I can't think of anyone I may ask on such short notice," said Madame Golitsyn.

"Very well," said Madame Koska. "We are a larger group this time anyway. I will see you there tomorrow night."

❈

As always, the Petrograd Room was the epitome of opulent elegance. The huge restaurant, with its tables arranged around the square dance floor, was decorated lavishly, the red and gold tints shining softly under perfectly balanced lighting. Each table was covered with a snowy cloth, and piled with traditional foods, candles, spring flowers, and, of course, a large basket filled with painted eggs as a centerpiece—each egg looking like a giant jewel. Madame Koska felt that the atmosphere was even more festive than the last time she and her friends assembled at the Petrograd Room. She knew that Russians loved Easter more than any other holiday, so perhaps that was the reason, but she acknowledged that it had something to do with her, personally. She was not under the dark cloud of suspicion and crime that had been so oppressive during that memorable dinner.

"Darlings, I am speechless! Look at all this food on the table—it looks like sweets and cakes!" said Wilma. "But it can't be since we have not had dinner yet!"

"It's going to be our dessert," said M. Danilov, smiling at Wilma who was sitting next to him. "This tall narrow thing is *kulich*, a Russian bread that is really more like cake. It will be eaten with *paskha*, this pyramid-like sweet. It's a kind of cheesecake. They might be offering baklava as well."

"Vasily, what do you think? Should we order our traditional meal?" said Madame Golitsyn. "I am sure our Russian friends would enjoy it, and our English and Dutch friends would like the novelty!"

"How I miss these celebrations in Russia," said M. Danilov, sighing dramatically. "The dear motherland..."

"No, you don't, Sasha, and I can't say that this heartfelt sigh makes me too sorry for you," said Mr. Korolenko with a smile. "You enjoy Easter and Christmas and what-have-you in the best hotels in Europe and the United States. You would not want to settle in one place, and you feel your creative freedom is not encouraged in Russia."

"Well..." said M. Danilov sheepishly, and everyone laughed.

"I can understand that," said Mr. Van der Hoven. "There is such joy in travelling the world."

"But you are not travelling anywhere!" said Gretchen, clutching his arm. "Never! At least, not without me making sure you are safe!"

Mr. Van der Hoven laughed and patted her hand. "No, don't worry, my little one. I am not going anywhere."

M. Danilov looked at Gretchen with professional appreciation. "You really should be in the theatre, Miss Van der Hoven," he said. "With your looks, you can go far."

"No, no. It's too late for the ballet, M. Danilov," said Gretchen. "I am too old to start dancing."

"But not too old to act," said M. Danilov.

"Miss Van der Hoven is studying at the university," said Madame Koska. "And vhen she completes her courses, she has an interest in fashion."

"Exactly," said Gretchen. "I want to be the best vendeuse in the best atelier in London!" Madame Koska smiled affectionately at the girl. "You vill go far in the vorld of fashion, my dear," she said.

The waiter came to the table, and after serious consultation, the dishes were chosen, since every course had the option of two or three traditional dishes. For the appetizer, they settled on potato and onion pancakes called *draniki*, served with sour cream and caviar; for the soup, they chose *rassolnik*, made from beef and barley and served with pickles; for the entrée, *kvass*-marinated pork loin baked in pastry and served with vegetables, and for dessert, the cakes already on the table.

"This is a lot of food," said Inspector Blount.

Natalya laughed. "You should have seen the Easter dinner I attended at the Tsar's court in 1903. The idea was to have forty-eight courses, each course representing a day of Lent. We had paskha, Easter bread, eggs, sturgeon, beluga caviar, salmon, pike-perch, pheasant, partridge, black cock, duck, lamb, bacon, tongue, beef, veal, and several kinds of pierogi, you know, the little filled pies."

"Good God," said Inspector Blount.

"Of course, no one ate *everything*," said Natalya. "You chose what you liked best. Whatever was left was given to the poor, so nothing was wasted. It's the idea of treats following abstinence. A tradition. I was there with other children, though, and we really ate so much; it was ridiculous. And we had glorious fights, each holding an Easter egg and banging it against the other children's eggs to see whose would be the last to break. Some of the adults joined as well."

"Natalya, while we are waiting, won't you give everyone their present?" asked Madame Golitsyn.

"Certainly," said Natalya, pulling a large basket from under her chair. It contained a collection of eggs, nestled on multicoloured, soft silk. They were not the usual dyed eggs. Each egg had been emptied of its content, cleaned thoroughly, drilled carefully in a special pattern, and then embroidered with colourful floss. The result was something that belonged in a fairy tale. Everyone gasped at the incredible creations, trying to understand how it could be done. Natalya handed them around, producing a little silk bag for each.

"They are considered good luck," she said. "Be careful not to break them! They should bring you a very happy year, Easter to Easter." Just as she was saying that, her own egg slipped from her hand and fell on the floor, breaking into tiny pieces. Natalya froze in terror, but it did not last. Her good sense made her overcome the superstition, and she laughed and said, "I'll just have to make another one for myself, so I can keep the wonderful good luck I already have!" And everyone relaxed. The waiters started to bring the dishes, and the serious business of Easter dinner had begun.

As they were finishing their after-dinner coffee, they noticed a slight commotion at the entrance. A police officer was talking to a waiter. The waiter pointed at their table, and the officer approached it.

"Inspector Blount," said the police officer, "I am sorry to interrupt, but Mr. Danilov must come with us, and you might wish to come, too. There has been a death at the theatre, Mr. Danilov."

M. Danilov stared at the police officer. "A death?" he asked incredulously. Madame Koska could tell he thought his poor English was making him misunderstand something.

The police officer looked at a paper he held in his hand. "Yes, one of the ballerinas, Miss Solange Forestier. She died on stage, at the end of the performance of the first ballet."

M. Danilov seemed utterly baffled. "Was there an accident? Did she fall, or did something fall on her?"

"No," said the police officer. He seemed to be uncomfortable and looked at Inspector Blount for help. The inspector shrugged helplessly.

"Was a doctor called? What is going on there?" insisted M. Danilov. "The girl was not sick, as far as I know."

The officer remained quiet.

Inspector Blount put his hand on the impresario's shoulder and said, "Let's go, M. Danilov. It will be best to get there right away and try to make sense of it. Korolenko, please come along, I may have to speak to some Russians..." They left the restaurant, while the others stayed in their seats in varying degrees of shock and surprise. Since most of them knew, or at least suspected, that Mr. Korolenko was working for the police, no one wondered about the inspector's request.

"I knew it was bad luck when the egg broke," said Natalya quietly.

"Now, now, Natalya," said Vasily, "there is no reason to make such connexions...it's superstitious. We will soon find out what happened, and in the meantime, let us say our Easter blessing, as we were ready to do after drinking our coffee. It is even more appropriate to do so now, in memory of Mademoiselle Solange. Most of us didn't know her, but we are all sorry for her passing."

"Indeed," said Madame Koska. "Please say grace."

"It is simple, as you know, my dear Madame Koska. *Christ has risen.*"

"*Indeed, He has risen,*" answered all those who knew the blessing.

"And may Mademoiselle Solange rest in peace," said Natalya. "I met her during her measurement session. A pleasant, cheerful young woman...it's so sad."

"Do you think she might have stumbled during one of those high jumps? Do people sometimes get killed performing in the ballet?" asked Wilma.

"I have never heard of any ballet dancer dying on stage," said Madame Koska. "In addition, she did not dance in *Giselle*, only in *Le Spectre de la Rose*, and the female dancer does not perform any high elevations in that ballet; only the male dancer does."

"It's extremely strange," said Mr. Van der Hoven. "Well, I think perhaps we should break up and go home… We can't help them, and there is no point in speculation."

"Yes," said Madame Koska. "Ve have finished anyvay."

"My dear friends," said Vasily, "please don't let this sad occurrence destroy the joy of Easter and the pleasure of having dinner together."

"No, of course not," said Madame Koska. "It is sad, but ve really must accept the good and the bad life hands us…and ve must return here sometime soon and celebrate another occasion."

"Last time we all went to church," said Wilma. "Can we go again?"

"There is no special service right now," said Vasily, "but of course the church would be open and extremely well-decorated. It's really a beautiful sight."

"Yes," said Natalya. "Let us go. It will be comforting." Mr. Van der Hoven and Gretchen also wanted to go.

"I am very tired," said Madame Koska. "I simply can't go to church and must leave you, my friends. I hope you don't mind."

"Of course we don't mind! You must go and rest, my dear Madame Koska!" said Vasily anxiously. "You work so hard…"

Leaving the restaurant, Madame Koska said to Madame Golitsyn quietly, "Would you like to come home with me? I expect Dmitry will call and let me know what happened…" Madame Golitsyn nodded, said something to her brother, and the parties went on their separate ways.

At home, Madame Koska poured tea. Neither of them wanted to eat anything after the enormous dinner, but holding the warm teacups could be comforting.

"I can't understand this situation," said Madame Golitsyn. "Mademoiselle Forestier got sick on stage, I imagine. But why did they call the police? Why not rush her to the hospital?"

"Perhaps a doctor saw her, someone who had been in the audience, and declared her dead," said Madame Koska. "A heart attack could kill even young people; I have heard it happens to players of several violent sports. They may be born with a weak heart, and no one knows until they die."

"Yes…" said Madame Golitsyn. "It's possible." She did not look entirely convinced, but had no other option to offer.

"I hope Dmitry calls," said Madame Koska. "He might tell us what happened; he probably has an idea already."

Madame Golitsyn smiled. "At least, Vera, I am glad you and Mr. Korolenko are together. I am so happy I introduced you."

"Yes," said Madame Koska. "Who would have imagined it could happen after all these years?"

"Do you plan to be married?" asked Madame Golitsyn.

"No, no. Much too early to even think about it," said Madame Koska. "Why should we?"

Before Madame Golitsyn could answer, the phone rang. Madame Koska went to the side table to pick it up, and Madame Golitsyn heard her cry out in dismay. She waited, terrified. Madame Koska put down the receiver and turned to her friend, her face white with horror.

Madame Golitsyn looked at her, saying nothing, observing that her friend could barely bring herself to speak.

"She was poisoned, Annushka."

"Poisoned? You mean the girl was murdered?" asked Madame Golitsyn, incredulously.

"They don't know if it is suicide or murder, but the signs of poison were clear as can be. And they know how she got it, too. It was the rose."

"What rose?" asked Madame Golitsyn, confused.

"Remember the rose that the girl smells after the Spectre disappears, and she wakes up? She picks the rose from the floor and smells it. You see, the poison was in the rose."

"But...would anyone commit suicide like that?" said Madame Golitsyn. "In front of an audience? Why?"

"Performers are sometimes a little strange when it comes to fame and adulation," said Madame Koska. "She might have done it as the last, spectacular show. The Grand Finale."

"Do you really believe it, Vera? Was the girl particularly sensitive, sad, melancholy? Or ill?"

Madame Koska thought about the simple, ordinary girl, a good dancer with a promise for a wonderful career, enjoying her adventures. She was a happy creature and did not seem to have a care in the world.

"No, Annushka. I don't believe she killed herself," said Madame Koska. "She was not the type."

"So it can only be murder," said Madame Golitsyn, shuddering at the thought.

"I am afraid so, Annushka," said Madame Koska. "But why?"

Five

Throughout the usual busy day at the atelier, Madame Koska could think only of Solange's murder. She went mechanically about her business, accomplishing her tasks with her usual efficiency, but she kept waiting for a call from M. Danilov. She assumed the impresario would continue with his plans, particularly since poor Solange was not part of the *Icarus* ballet, but she felt she needed to discuss the matter with him. He did not call. Madame Koska did not want to intrude by calling him so soon and decided to wait a day or two, but as she was going over the accounts, as she did every night after everyone was gone, she could not concentrate. Finally, she gave up, put the papers in the safe, and called Madame Golitsyn.

"Annushka, I need your advice," she said when Madame Golitsyn picked up the telephone.

"Would you like to come over and have dinner?" asked the hospitable Madame Golitsyn.

"That would be lovely," said Madame Koska. "Thank you. I am in a quandary about the murder, and I don't want to ask anyone else."

"Heavens, Vera, wouldn't Mr. Korolenko be the right person? He is much more experienced in such matters than I am," said Madame Golitsyn, surprised.

"Especially not him, Annushka. He works with the police, and it is much too early to involve them in the matter I have in mind. I was requested to keep it a secret, but I must have your opinion."

"Very well," said Madame Golitsyn. "I'll start dinner."

※

Madame Golitsyn's drawing room had a calming effect on Madame Koska whenever she visited. The way her friend had turned the modest apartment into a haven from the old Tsarist world never ceased to delight her. The piano, covered with its golden silk scarf whose long fringe reached the floor, the intricate and colourful floral embroidery on the black woollen shawl draped over the large sofa, and the old watercolours on the wall, all lent an air of comfort and security. The rose potpourri in the alabaster bowl gave its ever-present scent, and the brass samovar, gleaming softly over the white lace tablecloth, sang its timeless song. Madame Koska sank into a chair and felt herself relaxing.

The wonderful aroma of Madame Golitsyn's delicious chicken fricassee and potatoes au gratin drifted into the room from the kitchen, overpowering the potpourri. It was served with the perfect light wine, and followed by a small green salad. Over the coffee and cake, Madame Koska finished her story—recounting to Madame Golitsyn everything Galina Danilova had told her about her own illness, her need to go to Switzerland for treatment at the sanatorium, the possibility of her retirement, and the unusual relationship between Victor, Danilov, and herself.

Madame Golitsyn thought for a few minutes, sipping her coffee. "This is all quite serious, Vera, but I don't see the connexion between this story and the murder," she finally said.

"I don't understand the connexion either," said Madame Koska, "but I have a strong hunch that there is one."

"Then you must suspect something, Vera. Otherwise there would be nothing to attract anyone's attention. Yes, this is a strange relationship, though not quite a ménage à trois, and it is sad that Galina must stop dancing, but Solange was not involved with any of them."

"Yes, I do suspect something, but it's vague. The living arrangement of these three was a very straightforward relationship of convenience, and Solange was not part of it; it's something else altogether. It may be a wild conjecture on my part, but could it be that the murder was a mistake? That the killer's intended victim was not Solange, but someone else?"

"But it is well-known that only the girl in the ballet smells the rose!" said Madame Golitsyn. "How could anyone make a mistake?"

"The poison could have been dripped on the rose by accident. There may be another object that has the poison on it."

"Hmmm," said Madame Golitsyn. "If so, someone else might smell it by accident, whatever it is."

"That is why I am concerned," said Madame Koska. "For one thing, I think every rose on Victor's costume should be carefully checked."

"Vera, are you thinking that the intended victim was Victor?"

"It's more logical that someone is Victor's enemy than Solange's," said Madame Koska. "He is a star of such magnitude, that no doubt someone hates him. Revenge, jealousy, who knows? I'd like to know if there is a young, good male dancer waiting in the wings..."

"That should not be too difficult to find out."

"But I can't just go and talk about it to the police, or even to Dmitry, because I promised Galina Danilova that I would keep her secret. I strongly feel that this secrecy is a mistake, and that all the facts should be available to the police. What do you think? That is what I wanted you to advise me about."

Madame Golitsyn was again silent for a few minutes. Madame Koska waited. She knew that her friend valued discretion very highly; it was part of her nature and her upbringing, and the trust of a secret weighed heavily on her. But this was murder, and the rules were changed. Madame Koska lit a cigarette, placed it in a long ebony holder, and watched the grey smoke curling up to the ceiling.

"I think you should talk to Galina as soon as possible, tomorrow morning if you can, and ask her to talk to the police, even if Sasha Danilov feels it's going to affect his sales," said Madame Golitsyn finally.

Madame Koska sighed with relief. "I will do so," she said.

The next day, however, was so busy that Madame Koska did not find the time to call Madame Danilova. It was late afternoon before she managed to extricate herself from a whirlwind of fittings, orders, deliveries, and requests for appointments. Thank goodness Gretchen is still here until September, thought Madame Koska. But I must hire another vendeuse before she goes to the university. She sat down to look at the accounts when the doorbell rang. She opened it, and to her surprise, it was Mr. Korolenko.

"Dmitry, how nice to see you! I was not expecting you. Come in, sit down."

Mr. Korolenko sat on the chair across from Madame Koska's desk, leaned forward, and looked at her with some amusement in his brown eyes.

"Come on, Vera. You know more than you are telling me, I can see that."

"About what, Dmitry?"

"The murder. Don't try to look so innocent… You'd better tell me all you know, because someone you like may be in deep trouble."

"Who is in trouble?"

"Madame Galina Danilova. Inspector Blount suspects her of the murder. He did not say so yet, but he will, and very soon, too. I can see he takes the route of 'aging ballerina murders the young one who is about to replace her.'"

"Inspector Blount is an idiot!" cried Madame Koska.

"No, he is not an idiot. He may not see through walls, the way you do, my dear, but he is a good, solid policeman. And there is plenty of evidence against our Galina."

"Such as?"

"Such as the fact that she was the last one to be near Solange on her way to the stage, and in addition, she handed her the rose."

"But why? What was she doing there?"

"She often stays at the theatre and supervises for Sasha, seeing that everything is going well. She was probably giving a hand to the wardrobe lady."

"Anyway, that does not mean a thing," said Madame Koska. "There is plenty of evidence to show Madame Danilova did not have any reason to kill Solange."

"Evidence? What sort of evidence?"

"Well…" said Madame Koska, hesitating.

"Come on, Vera. What is the secret?"

"You are right; I must tell you. I did not want to since I was sworn to secrecy, but there is no choice."

After hearing the entire story, Mr. Korolenko said, "I tend to agree with you. In my mind, she is cleared. So who? And why? Solange was so harmless, and no one would gain from her death."

"I believe no one wanted to kill Solange. I think whoever put the poison on this rose intended to have Victor smell it and die on stage. I can't tell how he or she planned to make Victor smell the rose, since the Spectre never holds it, but that is less important than the motive for the murder."

"So we must find out who would gain from Victor's death."

"I have no names, but I suspect a certain group. Young male dancers do not have as many opportunities for advancement as female dancers. Look at all the ballets. One male to twenty, thirty females? Many ambitious male dancers never make a name for themselves. Is there someone at the Ballet Baikal who could be close to the position of principal male dancer if Victor was not there?"

"We must ask Sasha."

"This is very delicate, Dmitry."

"I know. We must navigate between Sasha's secret promotional designs, Galina's mysterious disappearance into a nameless sanatorium, Victor's terror of being murdered if he finds out, and a murderer who may or may not be dancing with poison in his hands."

Madame Koska laughed. "Not any worse than the previous case we handled, Dmitry. At least this time, I am not personally involved."

"I certainly hope not," said Mr. Korolenko.

To Madame Koska's surprise, Sasha Danilov received them calmly. She expected volatile emotions, drama, anger, fireworks, but nothing like that happened. M. Danilov directed them to a private room that was almost an office, where Madame Danilova was waiting. He closed the door and looked at them sternly from under his bushy brows. After a few seconds he said in French, as always, "I know my wife told you about her illness, Madame Koska."

"I hope you don't hold it against her, M. Danilov. I am entirely to blame," said Madame Koska. "You see, she noticed that I was puzzled about making two identical costumes for her and Solange. It seemed very strange, and I am afraid I was not discreet about it. Of course she knew I could be trusted."

"Technically you broke your trust, Madame Koska, by telling Dmitry, but I realise that you had no choice. Everything must come out into the open now... The Ballet Baikal will lose a great deal of money, but if the police really suspect my wife of murder, we have no choice but to make the whole situation public. The police will then leave her alone, I assume."

"Not necessarily, Sasha. Forgive me, Madame Danilova; I am not hinting that you are guilty! But the police do not usually think with great subtlety. Their line of thought will be that just because you are ill does not mean you were not raging against your successor," said Mr. Korolenko.

"So what is to be done?" asked Madame Danilova. "I really hope they will let me go to the sanatorium... I am very ill, Mr. Korolenko."

"They will certainly let you go to the sanatorium, but someone will be guarding you day and night, and because they suspect you, much time will be lost that should be spent on catching the real murderer."

"It's because of the rose, Madame Danilova," said Madame Koska. "If you had not handed the rose to Solange, they would have never suspected you."

"I do it so often, Madame Koska. Had I wanted to kill Solange I would have had so many opportunities. But where would I get poison? I know nothing about such things."

"We realise that, but to make the police agree with us, we may have to find them a more suitable suspect. You see, we don't think Solange was the intended victim. We think it was Victor. We believe the poison was actually used on his costume, or something else he owned, and it got on the rose by accident," said Madame Koska.

"I would like to send the costume to the laboratory for investigation," said Mr. Korolenko. "Can you get it for me?"

"Yes, of course. It may have been washed, though," said Madame Danilova.

"Traces would remain, enough to identify the poison, if it is there, Madame Danilova," said Mr. Korolenko.

"I will go to Wardrobe for the costume myself, at once," said M. Danilov. "I don't want anyone taking a chance." He left the room and

Madame Koska said, "Is there a young male dancer who may be jealous of Victor, Madame Danilova? Someone who might want his position so badly that he would be willing to commit a crime?"

"I doubt it," said Madame Danilova. "Leonard Bassin is the new protégé Sasha had recruited. He is very good, but he needs much training. We can call him, if you wish."

"Yes, please," said Madame Koska. "We will say nothing to alarm him."

M. Danilov came back with the costume, which was wrapped in a clean cloth and put in a bag. He handed it to Mr. Korolenko. "You can keep it as long as you like, Dmitry. Naturally, we won't have *Spectre* on again this season."

"Would you send Leonard Bassin here for a minute?" asked Madame Danilova.

The impresario started at the mention of the name. "Why?" he said. "What does he have to do with it?"

"Nothing much," said Mr. Korolenko. "We just want to be sure of that. Do you have any objections?"

"No, no...go ahead," said M. Danilov. But Madame Koska could see he was uncomfortable with this new development. Silently, he went out, and came back with a young man in training costume, obviously dragged away from a rehearsal.

Madame Koska looked at the dancer. He was almost a boy, probably eighteen or nineteen, and very handsome. He seemed to be shy and looked at the group with big blue eyes, round like those of a small child. Too innocent, she thought, noticing that M. Danilov was rather protective, keeping his hand on the boy's shoulder reassuringly. Hmm...she thought. "This is no longer a *ménage à trois*...more like a *ménage à quatre*... Could that be it? Jealousy between the impresario's favourites?" Involuntarily she glanced at Madame Danilova. To her surprise, Madame Danilova was watching her with a slight smile on her face. As she caught Madame Koska's eye, she nodded very quickly. No one else noticed, as far as Madame Koska could tell, but she was quite sure that Madame Danilova guessed her thoughts and confirmed them.

"M. Leonard Bassin, we are collecting information from everyone at the Ballet Baikal, regarding the death of Mademoiselle Solange," said Mr. Korolenko.

"But I was not there, Monsieur," said the boy. "I was not dancing that night."

"But you could tell me a little about Mademoiselle Solange, perhaps? Can you think of anyone who would have wanted to kill her?"

"She was very nice," said Leonard. "Always helpful to me. I am rather new, and so was she, so we were friends. I can't think of anyone who did not like her."

"So did you socialise? Did you go out together, maybe to eat or have coffee?" asked Madame Koska.

"Yes, we did. The night before she died, we went to have supper after the show. Victor came with us. They wanted to help me plan for the trip."

"Trip?" asked Mr. Korolenko.

"Yes, I am going to Monte Carlo to train with our school there. M. Danilov wants me to improve my technique because even though I get much help from Victor, he has little time between shows and rehearsals. I am supposed to leave next week and accelerate my training."

Madame Koska and Mr. Korolenko looked at each other, surprised.

"Why do you have to accelerate your training, M. Bassin?" asked Madame Koska.

"Because of Victor, Madame Koska," said M. Danilov. "Surely you know he wants to divide his time between dancing and choreographing? He is anxious to have Leonard improve to the point of being able to take his place in several ballets."

"No, I had no idea," said Madame Koska, and looked at Madame Danilova.

"I never thought to mention it, Madame Koska," said Madame Danilova. "I suppose I can't see what difference it makes, so it did not cross my mind. Does it matter?"

"Very greatly," said Mr. Korolenko. "Well, M. Bassin, you have been most helpful. We took too much of your time, but we are grateful."

"I can leave now?" asked the boy.

"Certainly," said M. Danilov, smiling at him. The boy left.

"He is clearly innocent," said Madame Koska, "and if necessary, we can communicate with him easily while he is in Monte Carlo."

"Of course," said M. Danilov. He seemed relieved. "Anyone else you wish to speak to?" he asked.

"I can't think of anyone right now," said Madame Koska.

"I'll take the costume to the police laboratory," said Mr. Korolenko.

"Wait," said Madame Koska. "M. Danilov, did you also bring the cap and the slippers? And the arm bands?"

"I brought the cap and arm bands, but he did not wear slippers," said M. Danilov. "He is dancing the Spectre role barefoot."

"Strange," said Madame Koska. "I remember pink slippers...no, wait, maybe I remember them from the first time I saw *Spectre*. In Paris, you know, with the original dancer."

"You might have also seen them when you came to the performance here," said M. Danilov. "Victor decided to dance barefoot only a few days ago, to get used to the way it feels, since he will be expected to do so in *Icarus*."

"Very well," said Mr. Korolenko. "Then I'll just take the package to the laboratory."

Six

Madame Koska and Mr. Korolenko were having a pleasant tête-à-tête dinner at her apartment when the telephone rang.

"Madame Koska, I am sorry to bother you at such a late hour," said the voice of Inspector Blount, "but I am desperately in need of reaching Mr. Korolenko. Is he with you? He is the only Russian translator I have."

"No trouble at all, Inspector," said Madame Koska graciously, despite her annoyance at being interrupted in the middle of dinner. She was the first to admit that a connexion with the police was quite helpful, especially when she had had to deal with the affair of the imperial brooch, but sometimes they were rather intrusive. She handed the receiver to Mr. Korolenko and left the room discreetly.

After a few minutes Mr. Korolenko joined her. "I have to leave right away, Vera," he said. "This is very, very bad."

"What happened?" asked Madame Koska, alarmed.

"Victor is in the hospital. They say he tried to kill himself," said Mr. Korolenko bluntly.

Madame Koska grasped the back of a chair that stood near her, her face losing much of its colour. "Was he saved?" she asked.

"Yes, he seems to be out of danger, but…"

"But you are not sure if it was truly a suicide attempt, are you, Dmitry?"

"No, I can't be sure. We don't know yet if anyone tried to poison Victor's costume, but if someone did, he or she might have struck again. I must go to the theatre to meet Blount."

"I wish I could come with you," said Madame Koska. "Galina…she must be distraught over this development. She could use my support."

"Of course you can come with me," said Mr. Korolenko. "Why not? Blount would be happy to have someone who could keep these divas calm."

They left the half-eaten dinner on the table, not removing the dishes—something Madame Koska would never dream of doing under normal circumstances—and went to the theatre. It was the end of the performance, and the audience, mercifully unaware of the events behind the scenes, filled the narrow street, blocking it and making it impossible for the police car to park in front of the theatre without making itself conspicuous by using the loud siren. Inside it was even worse. It seemed everyone knew about the attempted suicide. Dancers were running back and forth, some in costume, some in street clothes, not knowing what to do. Neither M. Danilov nor Galina were in sight.

"They may be at the hospital," said Madame Koska, speaking loudly, trying to be heard above the general din.

"No, they are here," said a voice next to her. Madame Koska turned to see Leonard Bassin, the young dancer she had met the other day. He was very quiet, but tears were streaming down his face.

"Victor was like a brother to me," he said. "I can't bear it."

"He is out of danger," said Mr. Korolenko kindly. "The police told me that."

"But he has lost his mind," said the boy. "He will probably try to kill himself again."

"Lost his mind? What do you mean?" asked Madame Koska. Her head ached with the noise, and she was not sure she had heard him correctly.

"He was always a little strange," said the boy. "He is different from other people. It's hard to explain. Victor is the dance, and the dance is Victor. He is only the dance, nothing else, he has no other thoughts, no other existence. Just the dance...but he is kind and sweet and loving..." The boy suddenly ran away and disappeared among the crowd.

Madame Koska looked at Mr. Korolenko, who was shaking his head. "I don't understand what he means," he said. "Victor is only the dance...what can he possibly be trying to say?"

"I do know what he means, Dmitry," said Madame Koska. "When I met Victor, he seemed vague. It's as if his thoughts are permanently elsewhere, and he is like an empty shell. When he dances, he comes alive. When he is not dancing, he is only half alive. He lacks personality when away from the ballet."

"But if he was always like that, why does Leonard Bassin say he has lost his mind?"

"I can't say. We must find M. Danilov and hear what he thinks."

Just as she said that, the massive figure of M. Danilov became visible at the end of a corridor. He shouldered his way through the crowd, pushing people aside, and with a few strides reached Madame Koska and Mr. Korolenko. "Come," he said. "Inspector Blount is with me." He turned around and they followed in his wake, the crowd dispersing to let them pass.

Inspector Blount and Galina were the only people present in the small room. When M. Danilov closed the door, the noise was greatly reduced, and Madame Koska felt better. She went over to Galina and pressed her hand with sympathy. Galina looked terrible. Her face was white as chalk, while two bright red, feverish spots lingered on her high cheekbones, a testament to her tuberculosis. Her high chignon was dishevelled, the hair showing traces of grey, which Madame Koska had not noticed before, and some of her black mascara was smeared under her eyes—or perhaps they were extremely dark circles. Galina pressed Madame Koska's hand in return, and gave her a grateful look. "I am so glad you are here, Madame Koska," she whispered.

"So what happened?" asked Mr. Korolenko with his usual calm. "And why did you need me, Blount?"

"I needed you because some of these dancers speak only Russian," said Inspector Blount. "We will call them soon. As for what happened, I think M. Danilov is clearer on it than I am."

"I found him," said M. Danilov. "He was not dancing tonight, so I did not know he was at the theatre, but I needed something in his dressing room and walked in. There he was, lying on the floor. He had been very incoherent for the last few days, behaving strangely...so I thought it was another episode. I bent over to talk to him, and realised something was very bad. I called the doctor right away, and he said it looked as if Victor had swallowed something. He was rushed to the hospital and they pumped his stomach. He took poison. They saved him with great difficulty."

"Another episode, did you say?" asked Inspector Blount. "What other episodes had occurred?"

"Galina witnessed the first time it happened," said M. Danilov. "I was not there."

"Yes," said Galina. "It happened a few days ago. He saw me coughing badly, something I had managed to hide from him for a long time. He looked at me with horror in his eyes and said, 'Are you sick? Your cheeks have these red spots like my mother had when she died.' I knew his mother died of tuberculosis, which is why it was so important to me to hide my own illness. Victor is so fragile, emotionally."

"So what did you say, and what was his reaction?" asked Inspector Blount, busily writing notes.

"He was frozen for a while, like a statue. Then he burst into tears; it seemed he could not stop sobbing. I held him in my arms and told him repeatedly that I am about to get the cure in Switzerland, in an excellent sanatorium. He did not seem to hear me at all. When he finally stopped crying, he sat on the floor and curled himself into a hunched position. I held his hand and waited for a long time. Finally, he looked up and blurted that his mother was too poor to get the cure, since his father had abandoned her for another woman. The usual tragic story, but now I understand better why he was always so afraid of losing the ones he loved. I asked him if he felt better, and he said that he did. I took him to his dressing room to rest, and he fell asleep almost instantly."

"And were there any other episodes?" asked Inspector Blount.

"Yes. He would wake up at night, screaming, but remembered nothing in the morning. During the day he was motionless, terribly quiet. He only came alive when he was dancing. He is not eating, either. Really, he eats practically nothing."

"Where he is getting the terrifying energy he still shows when he is dancing I'll never know," said M. Danilov. "He is almost like a machine now. But suicide? Why? Galina told him she was not dying, and he always believes anything Galina says."

"I wonder," said Madame Koska, and stopped.

"What about?" said Inspector Blount, looking sharply at her.

"Perhaps he heard a rumour that someone was trying to kill him, rather than Solange," said Madame Koska. "That would tip him over the edge."

M. Danilov suddenly looked very self-conscious and uncomfortable. "Ah, well, yes," he said. "I told him myself."

"What?" exclaimed Mr. Korolenko, for once shaken out of his self-control. "Have you gone mad? Why would you do such a thing, when we don't even know if the costume was poisoned or not? Didn't you realise that frightening him this way might cause enormous damage?"

M. Danilov did not answer for a long time, then raised his eyes to Mr. Korolenko and said, "I told him because I love him so much. I was terribly worried and wanted him to be careful."

"Sasha, how could you?" said Galina in quiet desperation. "You know how unstable, fearful, and fragile he has always been. Such a threat against his life would be too much."

"Bad decision," said Inspector Blount. "You should have consulted the police before divulging such a piece of information. I don't think you had the right to do so."

"I am sorry," said the impresario, and buried his head in his hands.

Madame Koska said nothing, but watched the impresario carefully. She had a sudden hunch that M. Danilov was acting a part; something did not seem right. She simply could not believe that this brilliant manager and manipulator of people could have made such a mistake. No, she thought. He had done it deliberately. But why? What could he possibly gain from destroying his star performer, the most famous dancer in the world, his prize?

She did not have much time to think about it. The inspector led Mr. Korolenko to interview several of the Russian dancers, and she was left with the impresario and Galina. Madame Koska decided to change the subject.

"It may be wrong of me to ask this question at a time like this, but M. Danilov, do you plan to go ahead with *Icarus*?"

M. Danilov raised his head and looked at her, genuinely surprised. "Of course I do," he said. "Why shouldn't I?"

Galina laughed, somewhat bitterly. "My dear Madame Koska, nothing will stop Sasha from going on with a ballet."

"But…Victor may or may not be able to dance, the two possible prima ballerinas are out of the picture… How will you handle it?"

M. Danilov waved his hand as if dismissing some trivial details. "There are always some difficulties, but they never stop me," he said.

Madame Koska privately thought that having a wife who is his prima ballerina afflicted by tuberculosis, her stand-in murdered, and his male star showing signs of insanity, may represent more than mere difficulties, but she refrained from saying so. She waited for him to continue.

"Victor will dance," said the impresario. "Even if his mind is not completely healthy, he won't give up his part. In the meantime, I will personally train Leonard Bassin as Victor's stand-in, just in case. His Monte Carlo training can wait. But Victor will dance, depend upon it."

"But the prima ballerina?" asked Galina. "Who will take my place? I simply must go to Switzerland, Sasha."

M. Danilov pulled a telegram from his breast pocket and smiled. Madame Koska did not like the triumph in his eyes. He handed the telegram to Galina, who took it silently. Madame Koska looked at it with her, and it contained one sentence. "Accept—stop—on my way to London—stop—Tanya" Madame Koska heard Galina gasp.

"I telegraphed her as soon as I heard about Solange's death," said M. Danilov in a self- congratulatory tone.

"But she walked out on you before, Sasha," said Galina. "She said she would not work with an established ballet, and she kept her word. She is either doing solos or has her own group."

"She accepted. You read the telegram."

"This is insane, Sasha. You will try to control her, and Tanya Lavrova does not accept any form of control. The two of you will fight and *Icarus* will be destroyed."

"I will let her do what she wants," said M. Danilov. "Or at least, make her think she is doing what she wants. It's worth it. She is a great dancer."

"She is the greatest in the world," said Galina. "But it will not do."

"Think, Galina," said the impresario. "The newspapers will say, 'For the first time, Lavrova and Parizhsky together!' I can just see the marquee with their combined names! Can you imagine? The audiences will be drawn like flies."

"I don't like it, Sasha, and I never will...but I am out of it, and of course you will do what you want." Galina sighed.

❀

"Annushka, he was practically licking his chops, like a cat," said Madame Koska. "He was so thrilled about the idea of Lavrova and Parizhsky together that he did not even pretend to consider Galina's advice or feelings."

Madame Golitsyn took a small sandwich from the tray. They were having tea at their favourite café, sitting in a corner by the great bay window, where no one could hear them.

"You know how he is, Vera," she finally said. "He has only one object, one thought. The ballet. People don't matter to him, at least not a great deal."

"I understand," said Madame Koska, "and I don't think it's so much the money as it is the glory of the ballet. He once said in my presence, 'People think of me as a money-grabber, a dishonest impresario who would do anything for success. But I am the antithesis of a money-grabber. I have no respect for money; not my own money, not other people's money. Mammon is not my god. I serve only one goddess—Beauty. For her, I will do anything.' And that makes him even more ruthless, I think, than a regular money-hungry, normal businessman. He is a zealot."

"Maybe he is the murderer, then," said Madame Golitsyn, smiling. "Maybe he did it so Lavrova can dance for him." Madame Koska looked at her, aghast.

"Vera, I was joking!" said Madame Golitsyn, alarmed by the look in Madame Koska's eyes. "I did not mean it seriously."

"I wonder," said Madame Koska, putting down her cup, since her hand was shaking. "I wonder. It's not all that far-fetched, Annushka. I can easily see Sasha Danilov committing a horrific crime if it served his purpose—or rather, the ballet's purpose."

"But if that is so, he never meant to kill Victor."

"You are right. If that is so, he meant to kill Solange. And he told Victor that someone might have wanted to poison him, despite the fact that he was asked not to tell him anything before the results came from the laboratory. I don't believe it was a simple mistake... It's possible that he wanted to create this diversion, to make Victor, as well as everyone else, concentrate on the attempt on his life, rather than on Solange's murder," said Madame Koska.

"It still makes no sense. Why wouldn't he simply write to Lavrova and ask her to come and replace Galina? What was the point of killing a stand-in who seemed so harmless and unimportant?" asked Madame Golitsyn.

"Perhaps there is something we don't know about Solange," said Madame Koska. "Could it be she had some power over him, blackmail, something like that?"

"His life is complex," said Madame Golitsyn. "Blackmail is always possible."

"I'll alert Dmitry to this possibility," said Madame Koska. "By the way, tomorrow I am going to meet Lavrova. She is coming to be measured for the costume. I hope we can adapt the one we started for Solange, since I am told that Lavrova is very small, even for a ballerina. If she is bigger than Solange, we may have to start a new one."

"I wonder what she is like," said Madame Golitsyn. "One hears so much about her, but most of it may be stories."

"Galina told me she is a very difficult person," said Madame Koska. "Driven, hard, cold, even cruel at times. No compassion for anyone. Yes, it will be interesting to meet Tanya Lavrova."

Seven

Early in the morning, Gretchen and Natalya stood at the front desk in serious consultation. Natalya, carefully turning around a beautiful hat, covered with shimmering, dusty rose silk, was shaking her head dubiously. "I don't know, Miss Van der Hoven…even the thinnest thread might cause a hole in this silk if sewn securely. And to sew three large roses to it is too much for such a delicate fabric. The silk will stretch."

"But Miss Saltykov, the hat is perfect for these two occasions, and I would feel silly to buy two identical hats and put roses on one. You would be the first to tell me not to be such a frivolous spendthrift."

"Yes, true, but I really don't know how to do it," said Natalya. "Perhaps Madame Koska will have a good idea."

"I know how to do it," said a quiet, musical voice. Both girls turned in alarm toward a petite woman who stood next to them. They did not hear her come in, and Gretchen was not even aware of opening the door to the public. The unknown woman smiled, and it was a totally bewitching smile. She was short, even for a ballerina, and very slim, giving the impression of an ethereal creature, lighter than the air itself. Her big black eyes and dark hair emphasised an extremely pale complexion.

"Don't be alarmed, the door was opened, and I stepped in," said the woman, amused by their expression. "I am Tanya Lavrova. I am here to be measured for a costume."

"Of course," said Natalya. "I am honoured to meet you, Madame Lavrova... I can start you right now, if you would just step in—but wait, here is Madame Koska!"

"Madame Koska, I am delighted to meet you," said the ballerina. "But I am not going anywhere before I show these nice girls how to fix their hat. You see, I use stage tricks even for matters of my regular toilette."

"Stage tricks?" asked Gretchen, intrigued. "Are they different from the adjustments we make when modelling?"

"It's similar to modelling tricks, I imagine, but necessarily more inventive and dramatic," said Madame Lavrova. "For example, when I danced the *Peacock's Romance* solo, I had to lose a tail feather toward the end of the show, so it would be left in the middle of the stage when I flew away and the lights went out slowly. It had to be secure while I danced, but fall away easily when I wanted it to do so, and no one should notice me doing it. You can do the same with your roses."

"This should save a lot of money," said Natalya, already thinking about her own hats.

"Yes. Instead of sewing the roses securely by using several stitches, or gluing them, you take a silk thread and pass it through the hat once, leaving a tail inside. Then, you pass it over and through the rose, crossing it between the petals, and through the hat again. You would now have only two threads on the inside of the hat, and you can tie them in a bow. Then, when the roses are no longer needed, you simply pull the thread, the bow falls apart, and the hat is hardly damaged, left with only two small needle pricks."

"Genius," said Gretchen. "I am sure I can find the absolutely perfect thread that will match each rose. Thank you so much, Madame Lavrova."

Madame Koska laughed. "Very nice!" she said. "I alvays say one should be resourceful and thrifty with one's vardrobe! Now, may I invite you to the dressing room, Madame Lavrova? Ve must measure you. Natalya vill take you there and I vill join you directly."

The ballerina floated after Natalya, and Madame Koska said to Gretchen, "She is tiny! Ve don't have to cut a whole new costume. Ve vill just adapt the costume ve made for Solange. This is really a time-saver, not to mention a money-saver for M. Danilov."

"So kind of her to help us," said Gretchen. "She is so famous, you would think she would not care about anyone else."

"Interesting," said Madame Koska. "I heard so many terrible things about her… Perhaps there are two sides to her character."

"Perhaps people are jealous," said Gretchen. Madame Koska mused for a moment. She did not think Galina, who truly disliked Lavrova, was jealous. But feuds between prima donnas were so common. She shrugged her shoulders. After all, was it her business how nice or not her clients were? She followed the ballerina and Natalya to the dressing room. As she went in, she stopped in surprise and stared as she saw Lavrova removing yards and yards of bandages from her legs, arms, and upper body. Natalya stood by, helping her to roll them neatly.

The ballerina saw her expression and laughed. "Nobody told you? Except for the time I spend on stage, or rehearsing, I must be wrapped in bandages to protect my poor muscles. They hurt all the time; I am never free of pain."

"And yet you dance as if it vere the most natural thing in the vorld for you," said Madame Koska, wondering. "Vhy are you always in pain?"

"I am too delicate for the hard work of ballet. My muscles are fragile and never grow very big no matter how much I work them, and my bones are brittle. Early in my career the doctors had advised me to give up the ballet, but how could I? It had always been my life, my soul, my entire being. I can't give it up any more than I can give up breathing," said Lavrova. "But medically they were right. Look at my legs and arms—they are much thinner than those of the average ballerina. And look at my feet."

Madame Koska looked at the small feet. She knew that every experienced ballerina had deformed feet, with bent or broken toes and many bruises that would never heal, but Lavrova's feet were in terrible condition; no one could dance on them without experiencing extreme pain.

"I see," she said quietly, "they seem to be bruised. Also, the arches of your feet are the most pronounced ones I have ever seen. Do they hurt?"

"Oh, yes, terribly," said Lavrova. "I actually put a piece of board in my shoe to force the arch to straighten a little. I had to fight for it; some people claimed it's cheating, that I had to take care of the position of the foot myself when I dance *en pointe*, and not use a crutch like that. But now many ballerinas use the board in their shoes."

"This is a most resourceful solution," said Madame Koska. "And that reminds me. Thank you for helping the girls vith the hat idea. It vas kind of you."

"I know what it's like to be young and poor," said the ballerina, with obvious good nature. "Life is sometimes very hard on women." Madame Koska decided that the ballerina could not be as bad as some people made her out to be. Could she ask Galina to elaborate? Or would it be an imposition?

At that moment Gretchen poked her head into the dressing room. "Madame Koska, Madame Danilova is on the telephone. Let me help Miss Saltykov while you speak to her." She smiled at Madame Lavrova, and noticing that some of the bandages were lying on an armchair, unrolled, picked one up and started rolling it as if it were the most natural thing in the world. Madame Koska smiled with appreciation. Gretchen was priceless in her total tact and discretion, and Madame Koska was going to miss her greatly when she went to the university.

"Madame Danilova, I am glad you called," said Madame Koska. "I am vorking vith Madame Lavrova; this is the first time I have met her, and I vanted to ask you something."

"What do you think of her?" asked Galina.

"She is certainly…unusual. But she seems pleasant enough. I am not sure vhat to think about her yet. That is vhat I wanted to ask you. Vas she really as mean as you said? She vas very helpful to Natalya and Gretchen, advising them about their own business."

Galina laughed. "You will soon enough get to know her better," she said. "She is changeable and moody. One moment, cheerful and even charming. The next, a tyrant and a threat. She was so utterly cruel to me when we were young."

"Vhat did she do?" asked Madame Koska.

"She came to the Mariinsky Theatre about a year after I joined, but was immediately promoted and advanced above me. I was not particularly resentful, this is the way of the ballet, and I was ready to accept her superiority. The director, Marius Petipa, was mad about her… But she never stopped taunting me about it, and I was not her only victim. She bullied and insulted the other girls. Not a day passed without her making someone cry."

"This is very significant," said Madame Koska. "A young girl, to act like that, she must have had a grave flaw of character." To herself, she started wondering if Galina was not, after all, still jealous at the early career slight. This was a complex relationship. She really needed to learn more before making a decision; she was not entirely sure why it mattered, but she had a hunch that something about it was important.

"Now, as a mature woman," Galina added, "I can see she was a driven, miserable, lonely creature. But as a young girl, all I saw was the pain she caused."

"On another subject, Madame Danilova, do you have news about your date of leaving for Switzerland?"

"Yes, this is why I called, Madame Koska. I am leaving in two days. I am so grateful to Inspector Blount. You see, I have no alibi, but the inspector does not wish to prevent me from going to Switzerland—with police escort, of course."

"Police escort? Surely he does not think you vould try to escape? For goodness sake, you are going to a sanatorium!"

"He has no choice, Madame Koska. He explained it to me, very kindly. And I don't mind. Whatever happens to me is no longer going to affect the ballet, so why should I care if an officer comes with me to Switzerland? He will be helpful on the way, and let's face it, there is a murderer at large. I feel secure to have police protection."

"This is true," said Madame Koska. "I did not think of it. But vhy are your movements of no interest to the ballet?"

"Because I am never coming back to the Ballet Baikal. Even if I end up with perfect health, I am tired of this life. I have sufficient money to live quietly—not a fortune by any means, but enough to allow me a comfortable lifestyle. I have reached the crucial point in life at which every ballerina realises that the time has come to stop dancing. Sometimes it's physical, sometimes emotional. In my case, both. In addition to the illness, I am truly disenchanted with Sasha's behaviour. He is callous. He does not care about me, or even about Victor, who is showing clear signs of mental illness."

"I understand," said Madame Koska, sadly. "M. Danilov is too obsessed with the ballet to see what he does to others. But I hope you and I vill remain friends, Madame Danilova. Vould you write to me and tell me of your progress?"

"Yes and yes, Madame Koska. We are friends, and I will write. When I come out of the sanatorium, I plan to settle in London permanently; this is where I belong. So we can see each other whenever we like."

"Thank you, my dear," said Madame Koska. "I vill expect to hear nothing but good news about your health! Take good care of yourself and be vell."

Madame Koska knew that Galina had no alibi; she was told that quite frankly by Inspector Blount, but she did not want to discuss it with the ballerina, afraid that she might hurt her feelings. She also avoided telling Madame Danilova that Mr. Korolenko explained that Danilov and Bassin gave each other an alibi. Apparently, they had spent the entire day together and so the preparations for Solange's murder could not have been done by either. Madame Koska smiled to herself about something else Mr. Korolenko had told her. Apparently, Inspector Blount was extremely embarrassed about the love affair between the impresario and the young dancer and could not bring himself to mention it directly to Madame Koska. Mr. Korolenko explained to him that Madame Koska was continental and sophisticated, did not worry about such relationships, and was aware of the relationship between Victor and Danilov. But Inspector Blount was still uncomfortable talking to her about it. Madame Koska made a mental note to tell Mr. Korolenko that the alibi was hardly valid—the impresario and the dancer may have been plotting the murder together.

She went back to the dressing room to see how Lavrova's session was advancing. Everything seemed to be in order.

"I am delighted that you vill be dancing in *Icarus*," said Madam Koska. "I vas afraid that vith Madame Danilova's health situation, M. Danilov might consider giving it up. It is such a magnificent undertaking, it vould have been a great pity."

"Give it up? Not Danilov. He knew I would be a thousand times better than Danilova, whom we all realise is fading," said Lavrova. Madame Koska, clearly surprised at such a cruel statement, looked at her with amazement. The ballerina laughed.

"I am a plain-speaking person," she said. "People say the most idiotic things about me...that I seem to be a fairy, a creature made of light and air, not of this earth. How funny I think it is. When I appeared at the Mariinsky Theatre, at the age of eighteen, the great ballet master, Marius Petipa, could not believe his own eyes. In all his long career, he said, he had never seen a ballerina perform quite like me, with such delicate charm. It's all nonsense, you know. I am a tough, hard, ambitious and determined person, and there is nothing fairy-like about me. I have a great technique, and I am a genius when I dance. But I am hardly a sweet creature of fantasy."

"I understand you were an overnight success," said Madame Koska, intrigued.

"Naturally. I went with the Mariinsky and Petipa to many countries in Europe, and then I left them because Sasha Danilov offered me a position of prima ballerina at the Ballet Baikal. Petipa was crushed. He could not believe that his beloved protégé could desert him. How silly of him to think I would care about him. When I left, he promoted Galina, but she was never as good a dancer as I was, and Petipa knew it."

"But you left the Ballet Baikal, too," said Madame Koska.

"Sasha was too domineering. He demanded obedience, but I am my own master," said Lavrova. "I have a mind of my own, and I would not have anyone manage my career and dictate to me where and when I would dance. So I became a true nomad, and travelled all over the world, appearing before royalty and in modest dance halls with the same dedication to my art. Royalty saluted me. At the dance halls and second-rate theatres, in company of jugglers and animal trainers, the audience had always gasped at the way I could make time stop as I dance."

"You are certainly honest," said Madame Koska, smiling.

"Yes, and why not be honest? The whole world admits I am the greatest ballerina of the age. There is only one dancer who is my equal—Victor Parizhsky, and he is no competition since he is a man. But it's not as simple as it seems. You see, Madame Koska, I am possessed. Or obsessed—I am not sure which. What I do know is that I have to do all that because I will not last. The audience thinks the dance is so easy, as if it costs me no effort at all, but I know that suddenly, one day, one night, probably on stage, I will suddenly collapse and die..."

"Heavens, Madame Lavrova, I hope not!" said Madame Koska, alarmed. She suddenly noticed that Gretchen and Natalya were standing as if frozen, frightened by the ballerina's revelations. What luck that Lavrova was not in London when the murder of Solange took place, thought Madame Koska. She could have easily been suspected of crime—a strange character, torn between so many contradictions and mysteries.

Eight

"You are assuming too much, Vera," said Mr. Korolenko. "You are convinced that Galina Danilova had nothing to do with the crime. What exactly are you basing this belief on, other than a very short acquaintance?"

"He is right, Vera," said Madame Golitsyn. "You have made up your mind about it without knowing all the facts about the murder. It is unlike you."

Madame Koska looked at them with surprise. "You believe Galina killed Solange?"

Madame Golitsyn shook her head. "No, we don't necessarily think that. But dismissing her involvement altogether, in any capacity, might prove a mistake."

"But my dear Annushka, why would you even begin to suspect such an old friend?"

"Because Galina had the best opportunity," said Mr. Korolenko, "and since we cannot decide on a motive, she must remain a suspect. She was the one who handed the rose to Solange."

"But what about motive?" asked Madame Koska. "Galina is too ill to dance and is planning her retirement. What was the point of killing Solange? And for our other option, the possibility that someone tried to kill Victor—I refuse to believe she would. He is like a son to her. And indeed, no competition."

"The motive could be something unrelated to her career. It may be personal," said Madame Golitsyn. She got up and walked to the kitchen to bring coffee and cake to the dinner table. Madame Koska looked at Mr. Korolenko thoughtfully. "Solange and Galina barely knew each other," she said.

"How do you know that?" said Mr. Korolenko. "The acquaintance might have been different from what you think."

"I don't understand," said Madame Koska.

"I am thinking about blackmail," said Mr. Korolenko. "What if Solange knew something that might have threatened Galina?"

Madame Golitsyn returned and sat down to pour the coffee and slice the cake. "Vera, do you know that Galina never had a single romantic relationship? Not even as a young girl?"

"No, I never thought about it," said Madame Koska. "She did explain to me her reasons for accepting M. Danilov's marriage proposal, and I understood that she preferred to give her entire life to the ballet. She said that a husband, or any personal life, would interfere with her career."

"It could be," said Mr. Korolenko. "But still, if you consider that on the one hand she was willing to live with two male lovers, and on the other hand she had no relationship with any man in her entire life, she might prefer relationships with women."

"I see…" said Madame Koska. "Yes, that is plausible. But such relationships are common in the world of the ballet, so would the revelation cause blackmail and then murder?"

"It's just one possibility," said Mr. Korolenko. "There may be others, but I think that dismissing her possible connexion is a mistake."

"I can imagine another scenario," said Madame Golitsyn. "She might have assisted someone else. Suppose Danilov had a reason to kill Solange—Galina might have helped him to do so."

"If that was the case, then every word she said to me about her situation with Danilov, her desire to leave the ballet, her retirement plans, were all lies," said Madame Koska. "She would then be a consummate actress as well as a great ballerina."

"Perhaps she is," said Madame Golitsyn. "I do find it hard to believe that my old friend would commit murder, but circumstances can sometimes drive people to horrific acts."

"I am more inclined to suspect M. Danilov is working together with Bassin," said Madame Koska. "I don't think that the alibi of being together the whole day of the murder could clear them of suspicion."

"Inspector Blount said the same thing about their alibi," said Mr. Korolenko.

Madame Koska drummed her fingernails on the table. She sipped her coffee and suddenly said, "Galina handed the rose to Solange. But who gave the rose to Galina? Or if no one did, where did she pick it up, and was it in the open so anyone could have poisoned it?"

"This is an interesting consideration," said Mr. Korolenko. "I don't know."

"I wish I could see the arrangements in the dressing room," said Madame Koska. "But how can I get in inconspicuously?"

"There is no point in going there," said Mr. Korolenko. "Sasha made it clear that they will not repeat *Le Spectre* this season, so the arrangement of the rose, the costumes, etc. cannot be seen."

"But Inspector Blount could ask them to reconstruct it," said Madame Koska. "And you are always with him to translate."

"Reconstruction will do no good," said Madame Golitsyn. "If Danilov is guilty, he would make sure the clues are no longer there."

At that moment the telephone rang. Madame Golitsyn spoke in Russian, but after several lessons with Mr. Korolenko, Madame Koska understood quite a bit and realised that her friend was talking to Natalya. "Yes, they are still here," she heard her say. "Of course, come right over."

Returning to the table, Madame Golitsyn said, "So as you probably heard, Natalya wants to see both of you. I told her to come; she did not want to discuss anything over the telephone."

Natalya came in shortly after, seemingly in a hurry and somewhat agitated. "I have been visiting with my friend, Lady Victoria," she explained. "She invited me to a soiree with excellent singing and playing; several prominent artists were to perform, so I did not want to miss it, and went. I am glad I did because I heard something strange which made me wonder about the murder of Solange Forrestier."

"From whom?" asked Mr. Korolenko.

"Leonard Bassin. He was there and said that he remembered me from the fitting we had a few days ago. He did not know too many people there, so he sat next to me when the singing was about to start. We were waiting for the music, when suddenly he looked around, leaned toward me, and said, 'I have something to tell you. Come outside to the terrace after the songs.' After the recital was over, I got up and went with M. Bassin to the terrace. He again looked around as if trying to be sure no one heard and whispered, 'You should tell your people that Galina Danilova has an arrest warrant waiting for her in Moscow.' And then he turned around and went into the room."

"Arrest warrant?" said Madame Koska. "Do you know anything about it, Dmitry?"

"No, I don't," said Mr. Korolenko. "I find it hard to believe. I assume if it were the truth, Inspector Blount would have told me."

"I followed M. Bassin into the room," said Natalya, "and asked him to explain the accusation. 'What's to explain?' he said. 'It's simple. She tried to kill another ballerina some years ago. She is crazy.' I told him that such a statement could get him in trouble if the facts were not proven, and he just turned around and left the house. So I decided I should go home and tell you."

"It is just as important if it is not true," said Madame Koska. "If he made it up, it's clearly to throw suspicion away from himself. I expect M. Danilov had no idea the little fool was spreading rumours."

"He is not very bright," said Madame Golitsyn, "but it may be that he pretends to be so simple."

"And we can't mention it to Sasha," said Mr. Korolenko. "If they worked together to murder Solange, it is best that he not know what Bassin said. But I must alert Inspector Blount."

"Yes, you should, of course," said Madame Koska. "There is something I can do, though, unless the inspector objects to it. I would like to go to Switzerland and visit Galina. I have promised her that I would visit if at all possible. I may be able to discover something."

"I don't think the inspector would object," said Mr. Korolenko. "Even if she is guilty, there is nothing she can do while in the sanatorium. And whatever she says, even if she lies, may throw light on the circumstances. I will speak to Blount."

❖

"I am glad you agreed to meet me, Miss Saltykov," said Inspector Blount. "And I hope it is clear that I did not ask you as part of the investigation."

"Oh yes," said Natalya. "I realised that. Naturally, we cannot discuss the investigation in public."

"It's not written anywhere in the rule books that a police inspector is not allowed to socialise. I hope by now we are friends and can just meet and relax over a nice dinner."

"It's quite the same for an embroiderer and beader at a fashion atelier," said Natalya, smiling. "We are allowed to go out! And yes, we are friends, despite our arguments over the affair of the Imperial brooch."

"The less said about the blessed brooch, the better," Chief Inspector Blount said. They both laughed. During that complicated case which had been the reason for their meeting, they were highly antagonistic to each other, complicating matters considerably.

"It's been quite an experience for me," said Natalya. "But despite all the troubles, I am grateful for having gone through it; the case changed me."

"If you mean how it changed your looks, Miss Saltykov, it was dramatic," said Inspector Blount, smiling. "But I am sure you mean more than that."

Natalya laughed. "Yes, it seems I was determined to look as terrible as I could. But the changes in my looks and thinking were interconnected. I owe everything to Madame Koska. She boosted my self-esteem by showing me I was an expert at my profession, not just an amateur, who would allow herself to be taken advantage of by every client or employer. And she helped me look a little better, which made me feel more confident when meeting people."

"You look more than a 'little' better, Miss Saltykov," said the inspector, looking with admiration at the aquamarine eyes and delicate face, charmingly surrounded by soft ash-blond waves. "And it seems that you have adjusted to your new life admirably."

"I love my new life, Inspector Blount. I believe I was in a state of perpetual nervousness and used the loss of my title as an excuse for my timidity. I would not go back to the old days even if I could. I am happy to be a professional, glad to be independent. I will always love the memory of the Tsarina, she was like a second mother to me, but I was a dependent, and now I am not. It's a joy."

"So in a way, it was a golden cage, Miss Saltykov. You do not belong in any cage—I think your freedom means more to you than anything else."

"Thank you, that is an insightful comment," said Natalya. "But don't you think it's time you started calling me Natalya?"

"With pleasure. And my Christian name is Brian," said the inspector.

"Cheers, Brian," said Natalya and raised her glass. The inspector clinked his glass to hers, and they smiled.

"You belong here in London with all of us, your new friends," said the inspector. "Also, it seems that you did not lose all your old aristocratic friends. I like the way Lady Victoria was determined to continue the friendship, despite your attempts to discourage her."

"I was silly, but it took me some time to grasp the idea that she was neither demeaning herself, nor doing me a favour. I finally understood the beauty of English society, where the upper classes do not disdain the middle classes. I love such fluidity."

"And speaking of Lady Victoria, I pursued your story of what happened there. I found nothing—and while we can't talk about it here, as we said before, I might just mention that Madame Koska's little holiday in Switzerland can be very useful."

"She is leaving tomorrow morning," said Natalya.

"I know how busy she is," said the inspector, "but when I mentioned the time she would be spending away from work, she dismissed it and said that this was more important, and it was her duty. Between us, Natalya, I suspect she enjoys sleuthing—and she is splendid at it. I will never forget her help during the affair of the brooch; it was invaluable. I wish I could recruit her to work for Scotland Yard."

"And make her stop designing clothes? Never!" said Natalya.

The inspector laughed and said, "Very well, she can continue doing it as a hobby, I suppose. I am most interested to hear what she will say after meeting Madame Danilova."

Nine

"Here are your tickets, Vera, compliments of Scotland Yard," said Mr. Korolenko, handing her an envelope.

"Why would Scotland Yard pay for my trip?" Asked Madame Koska, surprised.

"Because you are going on behalf of the investigation," said Mr. Korolenko.

"But I am merely visiting a friend," said Madame Koska, with some discomfort. "Besides, Dmitry, this ticket is for the Orient Express! Is it really necessary?"

"Blount suspected that if you go on your own, you might choose a less expensive way, and he believes that the Orient Express is the fastest, safest, and most reliable way for a lady travelling on her own. I offered to accompany you, but Blount felt that Galina would be more open to discussing these matters if the two of you were alone."

"This is true, Dmitry. She would feel it is an investigation, or that she is taking away too much time from our holiday. If I come alone, it shows that I want to spend time with her."

"Possibly. So you will go to Calais, then Paris, and from there to Lausanne."

"Yes, since Galina is at the Leysin sanatorium, it is not far from Lausanne. I know the area, and it is a simple trip."

❧

In past trips on the Orient Express, Madame Koska had always enjoyed the delicate balance between elegance and ostentation that the creators of the line managed to achieve. A waiter showed her to her table, and as she sat down, she remembered the amusing story of the maiden trip of the Orient Express in 1883. At the time, the waiters wore tailcoats, breeches, silk stockings, and powdered wigs, as was customary. The angry passengers demanded that the servers discard these wigs—the train's movement made the powder land in their food. Under normal circumstances, however, the ride was so smooth that the tables rarely shook and the plates hardly ever rattled.

The dining car was magnificent. The walls, hung with original paintings by several masters, were panelled with mahogany and teak, deeply tinted and polished to a soft glow. They were inlaid with delicate rosewood patterns and decorated with carved borders. The ceilings were painted with colourful images from Greek mythology. But the visual opulence did not interfere with the equally important attempt to make the travellers as comfortable as possible.

The tables were arranged on both sides of the car, next to the windows. On one side, they accommodated four diners. On the other side, only two; these tables were reserved for those who wished for a private conversation. Discretion was most important, since the Orient Express offered the preferred mode of travel to honeymooners, people on secret romantic assignations, high-level business meetings, legal and otherwise, and espionage. Royalty often travelled by the Orient Express, but they did not go to the dining car, since the company offered them private accommodations that were naturally even more luxurious than the rest of the train. On either side, the diners could place their belongings on racks stretching over the length of the car. They did not have to return to their compartments to retrieve cigarette cases, binoculars, or books when the meal was over, and they went to the drawing rooms to smoke or drink a glass of the best Cognac. As a subtle touch of assistance to those who badly needed it, the chairs were not attached to the floor as they were in many other trains. An overweight passenger could easily move his chair back and allow the proper distance to accommodate his girth. White damask covered the tables, the napkins were folded artistically, and each place boasted several crystal wine glasses. The cutlery was made from solid silver, as silver plating simply would not do. The gold-rimmed china was of fine porcelain and decorated with the company's crest, and of course, the cuisine matched the best hotels in Europe.

At the table, Madame Koska joined a lady who was travelling to Paris to shop, and an older married couple heading to Venice to enjoy the art and the gondolas. Pleasant, disjointed conversation lasted throughout the long meal, and as soon as they heard who she was, both ladies asked Madame Koska for a card and promised to come to the atelier.

Madame Koska decided to go to one of the drawing rooms; she felt she needed rest and some solitude. Settling herself in one of the comfortable fauteuils, Madame Koska took her cigarette holder and put a cigarette in it. A passing waiter stopped to light it, and as he moved away, she suddenly saw Leonard Bassin sitting in another chair. He did not seem to notice her and was absorbed in a newspaper.

Madame Koska was not sure what to do. Where could he be going? Why didn't Inspector Blount tell her that Bassin would be on the same train? Surely he knew! Would it be best to ignore Bassin and walk away? But how could she do that, both of them sitting in the same room?

Madame Koska got up, stepped right in front of his chair, and the young man raised his head and jumped to his feet.

"M. Bassin? May I ask vhy you are here?" asked Madame Koska pleasantly, in a non-confrontational manner.

"I... I... I am going away," said M. Bassin.

"Going avay? Did you get permission from Inspector Blount to leave in the middle of the investigation?"

M. Bassin looked at her, with a half belligerent, half fearful expression. "I have an alibi; I don't need permission," he said.

"That vas not my experience," said Madame Koska. "I had to ask his permission."

"I didn't ask," said M. Bassin. "I can do what I want."

"Very vell," said Madame Koska. "And may I ask vhere you are going? I am going to Lausanne."

"I am going to Paris and then to our school in Monte Carlo," said M. Bassin. "I want to take my training there."

"Oh, so M. Danilov sent you? That is a different story; he must have asked Inspector Blount."

"No, not really," said M. Bassin. "He didn't know I was going. But I left him a note at the hotel before I left."

"I see," said Madame Koska. "Sit down, M. Bassin, and let me explain something to you."

They sat, and Madame Koska said, "Don't be surprised if a police officer vill be waiting for you in Paris. M. Danilov vould caution Inspector Blount that you have left, because othervise, they vould suspect him of sending you without permission; such an act would put him in a terrible light."

"But we have an alibi!" repeated the young man feebly.

"Perhaps, but if I recall correctly, your alibi is for each other. So if M. Danilov allowed you to go avay, it looks highly suspicious."

"He can manage," said M. Bassin. "He can manage everything. I am not worried about him."

Madame Koska suddenly felt very, very angry with his carelessness and stupidity.

"Not concerned for him? Let me tell you something, young man. You are causing more trouble than you are vorth. You spread rumours, run avay, and altogether behave as if you vere guilty of the murder."

"I didn't kill Solange!"

"So vhy are you running avay?"

"Because I am scared," said M. Bassin. "Someone killed Solange. Someone tried to kill Victor. Now it will be my turn, and someone will try to kill me. Maybe you will try to kill me? Perhaps you are following me on this train?"

Madame Koska was quiet for a minute, thinking. The whole thing did not make sense. His reason for going to Monte Carlo was much too vague. "I am sorry, M. Bassin. I find it hard to believe you."

"So do I," said a voice behind her. A stranger rose from another chair and approached them. "May I introduce myself? I am Constable Jamison, here on the orders of Inspector Blount. I have been following you since you left the hotel in London, M. Bassin. When we reach Paris, I am taking you back to London."

"But you can't arrest me! I have done nothing!"

"I am not arresting you unless you refuse to come back to London. If you create difficulties, I have the authority to do so; you have disobeyed Inspector Blount's orders since you left London in the middle of a murder investigation."

"I won't go! I am going to Monte Carlo!"

"Constable Jamison," said Madame Koska. "I think it vould be a good idea to check M. Bassin's ticket. I have a hunch that he is not going to Monte Carlo at all and has another destination in mind."

"Indeed, I will. M. Bassin, please give me your ticket," said the constable.

M. Bassin turned abruptly and tried to leave the car, but the constable laid a heavy hand on his shoulder and made him stop. "I suggest you stop making difficulties, sir. You are incriminating yourself," he said.

M. Bassin sighed, pulled his ticket out of his pocket and handed it to the constable, who glanced at it and said, "You were right, Madame Koska; the ticket is to Lausanne. M. Bassin, you are under arrest. Kindly follow me to your compartment, where you will stay until we reach Paris."

"Vait a moment, Officer," said Madame Koska. "M. Bassin, vhy are you going to see Madame Danilova?"

"Because I wanted to find out if she was the killer," said the young man, gazing at the floor.

"Or perhaps you intended to kill her, M. Bassin?" said Madame Koska, disgusted. The young man did not answer.

"I will bring him to Inspector Blount, Madame Koska," said the constable, shrugging. "Let him sort it out."

Madame Koska went to her compartment. It was a private one, designed for a single person, as requested by Inspector Blount for safety reasons. It was luxurious and welcoming, and the attendant already transformed the daytime sofa into a comfortable bed. But she was too tired and dispirited and did not enjoy it as she would have otherwise. Nor could she sleep well.

"My dear Vera," said Madame Danilova. "How wonderful to see you. I can't tell you how happy I was when I got your cable."

"And I am glad to see you, especially as you look so well already. The staff must be taking excellent care of you here."

"I do feel much better," said Madame Danilova. "I think the cessation of the extreme tension I felt in London is significant to my recovery."

"Modern medicine is inclined to think that states of mind affect the body," said Madame Koska.

"Are you comfortable? I hope you are not cold," said Madame Danilova, anxiously. "We are supposed to spend hours in the cold air." They were sitting on a spacious veranda lined with comfortable beds. A few patients rested there, the others presumably taking the air and sun cure on their private balconies. All of them were wrapped in warm blankets since the dry air was cold.

"I am perfectly comfortable," said Madame Koska. "They advised me to bring a warm coat, and Annushka made sure I took this thick Russian shawl. I have another one here in this parcel—Natalya embroidered it just for you with traditional bright flowers." She spread it over Madame Danilova's blankets.

"Dear, sweet women," said Madame Danilova, gazing at the lovely gift. "It is such a comfort to know that three such wonderful friends like you will be there when I settle in London."

"We will be waiting to welcome you, Galina. We can't wait to have you come back," said Madame Koska. Looking at the thin, beautiful face, she was again entirely certain that Madame Danilova was innocent. So certain, in fact, that she decided to change her tactics and not try to conceal the details from Madame Danilova, but be honest with her.

"And how is the investigation going?" asked Madame Danilova, as if reading Madame Koska's thoughts. "Is there any news?"

"I have much to tell you, but do you think you are well enough to discuss it?"

"Yes, I am," said Madame Danilova. "And I feel more detached, less involved. I am even less worried about Victor. I know he is mentally ill, and I can face it. He needs help, and he will get it, and there is nothing else I can do for him."

"This is an excellent attitude," said Madame Koska. "Tell me, how do you feel about Leonard Bassin?"

"I have little interest in him. He is very young, quite silly, and I wish him no harm, but I can't say I like him. He is not a bad person, not evil, but he is an opportunist and has no ethics. I have seen him behave in petty, envious ways, and he is quite prone to spreading lies and rumours. He is probably like that because of the terrible life these boys have—I told you Victor's story. They all live like that, and it affects them."

"Lies and rumours?" asked Madame Koska.

"Yes. I am sure you know what Bassin said about me, for example. He thought that I was trying to persuade Sasha to drop him and restore Victor as his lover. So he started saying that there is an arrest warrant against me in Moscow. But he changes the reasons for the warrant as needed. When suspecting I was damaging his romance, the reason for the warrant was that I seduced extremely young ballerinas. These days, it is because supposedly I murdered a ballerina there."

"So you are aware of these rumours. Interesting. Yes, Bassin told Natalya that you had murdered this ballerina."

Madame Danilova laughed. "I hope no one takes him seriously," she said. "Can you imagine me seducing young girls and then murdering them? What next? He may suggest I have embezzled money so Sasha would get rid of me."

Madame Koska laughed. "Well, try to get well and come back quickly," she said.

Ten

"The sanatorium is a strange place," said Madame Koska.

"In what way?" asked Inspector Blount.

"On the one hand, it is much like a luxury hotel; comfortable, elegant rooms, highly attentive staff, admirable cuisine. On the other hand, the atmosphere is morbid, permeated by a profound sense of illness."

"It is a hospital, after all," said Madame Golitsyn, getting up to refill the tray with more pastry.

"They try to disguise it. For example, people are alvays dressed beautifully for dinner, even vearing expensive jewellery." Madame Koska sipped her tea thoughtfully. "And yet, you see them carry these horrible hygienic blue bottles vhich they must use instead of handkerchiefs, vhich are inadequate for the symptoms of their illness. They usually conceal the bottles as best they can, but it is not alvays possible. And no matter vhere you are, you hear them cough. It is sad."

"But she is getting better," said Mr. Korolenko.

"Yes, she is definitely getting better. I made some discreet inquiries, and the doctor told me they are most optimistic about her recovery. She is compliant—drinks her milk, listens to the doctors' slightest advice, and never complains about the long hours she must spend lying down on the veranda. And it's so cold out there despite the bright sunshine. She loved the shawl you embroidered, Natalya. She used it all the time and said it vas so varm and beautiful it kept cheering her up every time she looked at it or touched it."

"I am so glad," said Natalya. "To be so ill and under a cloud of suspicion as well is terrible. Such a burden." She threw an angry look at Inspector Blount, who pretended not to notice it.

"Her mental state is much better as vell," said Madame Koska. "She told me she is feeling detached and even disconnected from her life at the ballet; surprisingly, she accepts Victor Parizhsky's mental illness with equanimity."

"I heard this is a common reaction to being isolated in a tuberculosis sanatorium," said Madame Golitsyn. "A friend who spent six long years in one told me that the mountains are so majestic that they become the entire world for the patients. They inspire an otherworldly feeling; common human problems become insignificant, even life and death are treated in a different way, becoming less important."

"I am not sure she vent so far yet," said Madame Koska, "but I vas happy to hear her make fun of Bassin's accusations; she did not take them seriously."

"We made inquiries, of course," said Inspector Blount. "There is no arrest warrant against Madame Danilova in Moscow. In other words, she had never murdered the alleged ballerina Bassin was talking about."

"Nor did she try to seduce any young ballerinas," said Madame Koska. "According to the first accusation Bassin made against her, she tried to do so in Moscow. His story changes according to his vhim or need."

Inspector Blount stared at her with utter disbelief. "He said that? This is preposterous. To me he only mentioned the murder. I am keeping him in custody until everything is sorted out, anyway."

"To me it seems he has done something so wrong that even after everything is sorted out, as you say, he needs to pay for it. Lying and implicating another person in a murder case would be considered a crime under the Tsar," said Natalya indignantly.

"Of course," said Inspector Blount. "I am not going to let him get away with it, you may be certain of it. He was doing his best to hurt Madame Danilova, and English law does not allow such behaviour any more than Tsarist law."

Natalya smiled with relief. "I am so glad of it," she said. "Normally, I am not terribly vindictive. But this malevolent creature really makes me angry. You should have seen how he behaved at Lady Victoria's party. As if he knew everything."

"Vhat did Danilov say when you told him about Bassin's lies?" asked Madame Koska.

Mr. Korolenko laughed. "He nearly exploded with rage. Bassin is lucky to be in custody, Danilov wanted to thrash him."

"Danilov is another matter," said Inspector Blount.

Madame Koska looked at him, surprised by his serious tone.

"You don't think, Inspector…"

"I have no proof," said the inspector. "But to me he is now the chief suspect. All these boys are his creatures, they blindly follow his orders. I would not be one bit surprised if he put Bassin up to his lies and accusations, and even arranged for his escape, so as to make matters more complex and further away from himself."

"But why would he wish to murder Victor Parizhsky?" asked Mr. Korolenko. "We were all under the impression that Solange was murdered by accident, and it was Victor who was the real target."

"It could have been Solange all along. I think he wanted to implicate Madame Danilova in her murder and get rid of both of them at the same time. Remember, he still does not know that she plans to retire. He probably thinks that she would be a disadvantage to his Ballet Baikal. A weakened performer, less attractive to the public every day, insisting on staying on as prima ballerina. She would cost him a fortune. Solange was of no importance to him. I don't understand ballet, but they tell me she was not good enough to be a prima ballerina, ever. So by removing her, and implicating Madame Danilova, he would achieve the goal of hiring Madame Lavrova," said the inspector.

"It makes sense," said Madame Koska. "He vould put the interests of the ballet ahead of his lukewarm affection for Galina."

"And so he orchestrates, or choreographs, these chaotic scenes to distract us from the reality of what he is doing," said Mr. Korolenko. "Yes, it is possible, I can't deny it."

"I never liked him, as you all know," said Madame Golitsyn, "but to do so much evil just in order to hire another ballerina? Isn't it a little far-fetched?"

"It's not just another ballerina," said Madame Koska. "Lavrova is more a phenomenon than a human being, as far as the public is concerned. She is legendary. And the lure of having her dance vith Victor, who is also a phenomenon, vas too much for him to resist. So here vere so many loose ends that he knew he could tie up—vith one murder. And perhaps…" she thought for a moment, and then said, "perhaps he knew that the only vay to lure Lavrova to join the Ballet Baikal was to create high drama."

"And you think he is capable of murder?" asked Natalya, shuddering.

"I have no doubt that he is capable of it," said Madame Koska. "Given the opportunity, Danilov could commit any crime for the ballet. But I vould have to be convinced that he really felt he needed to get rid of Galina. Does he or does he not know that she plans to retire? If he knew, he had no reason to do anything, just wait for her announcement."

"We must find out," said Mr. Korolenko. "Blount, should I confront him? As an old friend, tell him that he is a suspect and something must be done to clear his name? He surely realizes now that the alibi he and Bassin have together is not very strong."

"Good idea," said Inspector Blount. "Yes, go and talk to him, Korolenko."

"Vera," said Mr. Korolenko on the telephone, "I have news, and we need to confer. Inspector Blount has positive results from the police laboratory, and M. Danilov has an interesting plan for which we need your help. Also, I saw Danilov."

Since Madame Koska was at the front desk, and a client was just entering, she could not talk freely.

"Vhere and vhen do you vish to meet?" she said carefully, knowing that from the way she spoke, Mr. Korolenko would understand that they could be overheard.

"I think it would be most discreet if the inspector and I come to your apartment this evening, after dinner," said Mr. Korolenko. "Besides discretion, we don't want to interfere with your work day." It made sense; she really could not afford to keep running to the police station, thought Madame Koska. "Very vell," she said. "Is anyone else coming?"

"We may telephone M. Danilov," said Mr. Korolenko. "He may be available after the show. I will see you tonight." He hung up the phone.

Madame Koska shook her head, apologised to the client, and plunged again into her busy day at the atelier. So many ladies needed a new summer wardrobe… The atelier was full of delicate chiffons and silks for evening gowns, pure white linens and batistes for day wear, and boxes of artificial flowers, laces, and ribbons. The horrible crime mercifully receded from her thoughts.

❦

Around ten o'clock in the evening, Madame Koska received Mr. Korolenko and Inspector Blount with her usual poise, aptly hiding her fatigue. She invited them to sit down and inquired if they would have tea or a glass of wine. Both declined any refreshments and proceeded to business directly.

"The results, I understand, are positive?" asked Madame Koska. "Are they certain?"

"Yes," said the inspector. "They found a small amount of strychnine, of the same type that killed Solange, on the costume. Very little, but enough to identify it. Of course you know Victor Parizhsky also swallowed strychnine."

"In other words, gentlemen," said Madame Koska, "there is no doubt that the murderer had made the attempts on both Solange and Victor."

"But it was not Danilov," said Mr. Korolenko. "When I confronted him, and told him he was the chief suspect because of his desire to hire Lavrova, he looked at me as if I was insane and asked me why he should bother to do anything so dangerous when it was perfectly clear that Galina was retiring. I asked him how he knew it, and he said that anyone with half a brain could tell that she would never be able, or willing, to dance again."

"It certainly points that way," said the inspector, "I am almost assured that the murderer wanted to kill them both. But we have no idea who, or why. Also, we still are unable to verify with any degree of certainty if Victor Parizhsky tried to commit suicide or was poisoned by someone else."

"However," said Mr. Korolenko, "a new situation may help us toward some discoveries, and for that we will need your help, Madame Koska."

"Vhat is it?" asked Madame Koska.

"I don't know if you are aware of it, but Danilov had never let anyone film Victor's dancing. He had allowed other people to be filmed, but for some reason, not Victor."

"Probably his vay of creating mystery," said Madame Koska. "The only vay anyone can see the great Parizhsky is on stage... It's all about money."

"Yes, but now that Lavrova is here, he decided it would be a good promotional idea to create a record of Victor and Lavrova dancing *Le*

Spectre de la Rose. Of course he claims it is just for posterity. The two greatest ballet dancers in the world, together, for the first time."

"But Victor is in the hospital. Vould the authorities let him go? And even if they did, could he dance, in his mental state?" asked Madame Koska.

"You know Sasha," said Mr. Korolenko. "He will persuade the authorities to release Victor for a couple of rehearsals and for the filming. And if he tells Victor to dance, Victor will dance. He obeys Danilov like a puppet on a string."

"Does M. Danilov know about the poison on the costume?" asked Madame Koska.

"Not yet. We are going to telephone him right now."

"But...isn't it dangerous? Vouldn't the murderer try to kill Victor again?" asked Madame Koska.

"Yes, it is dangerous," said the inspector. He looked embarrassed. "Well...this is where we need your help, Madame Koska. You can ask M. Danilov to allow you to come to the filming."

"Vhat kind of excuse can I make? They don't need costumes for *Spectre*!" said Madame Koska.

"That you wish to see Lavrova dance. It would help you design her costumes," said Mr. Korolenko.

"And vhat should I really have to do?"

"Mostly, watch the performance, look for clues on stage to the murder," said the inspector. "You will have a unique opportunity to sit near the stage."

"I see..." said Madame Koska. She was quiet for a moment. "Yes, I see vhat you mean, Inspector. Yes, I vill certainly be happy to attend this performance. Cigarette, gentlemen?" And she pulled out her long cigarette holder, offering them her cigarette box, deep in thought.

M. Danilov seemed glad to see Madame Koska when she visited the next day. He led her to a small, dusty room, its atmosphere full of cigar and cigarette smoke. She sat on a hard chair by the large wooden table which was covered with old props. She mentioned the filming, pretending great satisfaction that he was accomplishing it, and asked if M. Danilov thought Victor would be allowed out of the hospital for the filming and the rehearsals.

"He does not need any rehearsals," said M. Danilov irritably. "He will just need to come to the theatre an hour earlier, and warm up with the usual exercises. He knows *Spectre* perfectly."

"And you are sure they vill let him out of the hospital?" asked Madame Koska. "I heard some pretty sad rumours about how fragile he is, M. Danilov. They say that he just sits quietly all day long, either daydreaming or drawing unpleasant pictures of large dark eyes. Galina told me the pictures vere intended to make people stop vatching him all the time, vhatever that means."

"He is better, the doctors told me," said M. Danilov. "Besides he wants to dance so much that the doctors think it actually may help him recover."

Madame Koska doubted the information, which she suspected was Danilov's wishful thinking. However, she said nothing and just nodded.

"Galina spends too much time and efforts worrying about things she should stop thinking about," continued M. Danilov. "She should concentrate on relaxing and getting well. I have the situation well in hand."

He knows, thought Madame Koska; he does not really care. What a heartless creature he must be.

"And what can I do for you, Madame Koska?" asked the impresario, clearly trying to change the subject.

"Only that I vould appreciate it if you vould allow me to attend the filming," said Madame Koska. "It's a rare opportunity to see Madame

Lavrova dance, vhich vould be so helpful for designing her costumes; her unique style vill influence the vay ve sew the costumes."

"Certainly," said M. Danilov. "Anything to help you along, Madame Koska. I will let you know the exact time; we plan to do it as soon as I can hire the film crew." Madame Koska was surprised M. Danilov showed no objection and accepted her excuse, which to her seemed quite flimsy. One simply did not know with M. Danilov.

On her way home, Madame Koska thought about the last telephone call she had from Galina, just before she left for Switzerland. How different from her husband, how caring she was.

"Vera, I want to ask you a favour," she had said quietly on the phone that day. "If at all possible, would you keep an eye on Victor? I am terribly worried about him."

"Of course," said Madame Koska. "At least, I can try. I don't know if he trusts me."

"I told him to come to you if he is in trouble," said Galina. "Forgive me for presuming, but I knew you would help."

"It is perfectly all right," said Madame Koska. "He listens to you. Does he know you are leaving so soon?"

"No... I could not bring myself to tell him. A few more days at the hospital, I hope, would give him some strength to accept the fact, so I decided to leave it unsaid. He knows I have to go, but not the exact date."

"So stop vorrying, Galina. I am sure M. Danilov, even vhen obsessed, vould not harm Victor."

"I wish I could be sure about it," said Galina. "But now, when it is possible that Victor's useful days are over because of his mental state, and there is a new star in Sasha's life, I fear he simply won't care. Well... I have done all I could. I will soon write to you, and I hope you will be so kind as to write back and let me know how Victor survived the filming."

"Of course I vill," said Madame Koska. "Ve vill communicate regularly."

At least, thought Madame Koska as she was returning to the atelier, Galina was more relaxed at the hospital and hopefully recovering. It would be lovely to have her in London.

Eleven

As it so often happens, the call about the filming came at a very bad time. Madame Koska was in the midst of a consultation with a very important client—a wealthy member of the nobility—who had ordered an entire summer wardrobe. One of the dresses, a deliciously soft, white chiffon, had to be heavily beaded over the entire bodice and tiny cap sleeves. Natalya, as chief beader, was sitting with Madame Koska and the customer, looking at several intricate sketches of beading patterns. Deciding in advance what quantity of beads would give the necessary opulent look but still not pull the fabric with its weight, was not easy.

"I suggest making a small sample," said Natalya. "I really can't tell how many beads would start pulling the fabric down."

"But won't it take a long time?" asked the customer anxiously.

"Not vhen Miss Saltykov does the beading," said Madame Koska. "She is very fast. In the meantime, ve can start cutting the other dresses."

At this moment, Gretchen entered, and told Madame Koska that M. Danilov wished to speak with her. Madame Koska apologised to the client and went to the telephone.

"We will be filming tomorrow afternoon at one o'clock," said M. Danilov. "This is the only day the film crew is available. Do you still wish to come?"

Madame Koska thought for a moment. She really was terribly busy at the atelier. However, not only had she promised the inspector to be at the filming, but something was tugging at her consciousness. She was certain she would discover a clue, whatever it would be, at the filming. Still, she would have to rearrange some of her appointments. This would be most inconvenient. She drummed her fingernails on the table and said, "Yes, I vill be there." She sat at the front desk for a few minutes, musing. Then she picked up the phone and called Inspector Blount, who answered the call himself, an uncommon occurrence.

"Inspector," said Madame Koska, "the filming is tomorrow at one o'clock. There is one or two things I vanted to arrange vith you before I go."

"Yes? What would you like me to do, Madame Koska?"

"I vould like you to be at the filming, unknown to anyone, and bring a man vith you," said Madame Koska.

"I can do that, of course," said the inspector, "but why? Have you discovered something new?"

"No. But I have a hunch that there vill be an arrest during the filming."

"Very well, Madame Koska. I will also bring Korolenko, just in case the person I arrest speaks only Russian."

"Thank you, Inspector Blount."

"When we last worked together, I learned to respect your hunches," said the inspector.

Madame Koska laughed, a little apprehensively. This hunch promised nothing but sadness and trouble.

On her way to the theatre the next day, Madame Koska stopped at the atelier. "Miss Van der Hoven, I am leaving now. The afternoon should be quiet since ve rearranged all the appointments, but I am sure you vill be able to handle anything that happens."

Gretchen nodded distractedly and gazed at Madame Koska, musing. "Why are you dressed all in black on such a lovely afternoon?" she asked. "I would have thought beige, or dusty rose. Why all black so early?"

"I don't know," said Madame Koska. "I suppose I vas in a sombre mood. I am apprehensive about the ballet. Seeing *Le Spectre de la Rose* on the same stage vhere Solange vas killed. Still, you are right, but I have no time to go upstairs and change."

"I know what to do!" said Gretchen. "Miss Saltykov showed me several hats that came as samples. One of them is a pretty cream cloche with a large pink rose." She ran out of the room and came back with the perfect hat. With Madame Koska's white gloves, the outfit became lively and appropriate.

"Very nice effect," said Natalya, who had followed Gretchen into the room. Madame Koska felt her mood improving, and she cheerfully thanked the girls and went on her way, but she could not really shake off the apprehension and unpleasant expectations.

❀

The theatre was dark and empty, since only the first row was expected to be occupied when the dance would begin. For the moment, everyone was on stage, in preparation. The film crew were pacing back and forth, measuring some distances and fussing over the placement of certain objects. M. Danilov stood at the center of the stage with Tanya Lavrova, discussing last-minute details. The musicians were already in the orchestra pit, tuning their instruments to perfection. Madame Koska wondered how the sound of music would be recorded, since she had no idea how films were made. She looked into the dark cavern where normally an elegant, lively audience would be gathering, chatting, and laughing. The silence of the empty theatre was, in contrast, quite eerie.

Turning around, she saw that Victor had come on stage. He seemed his normal self, she thought, a bit vague as always when not dancing, but certainly neither haggard nor faint. Madame Koska felt relieved—obviously, the medications and rest were helpful to the young man. She hoped he would recover and be able to dance for many more years. He was attired in the freshly cleaned pink costume, into which all the roses were reattached. Of course he would do the usual and lose a few roses and petals on the floor, thought Madame Koska, amused. It was a charming part of this wonderful *pas de deux*, and M. Danilov would love to have it filmed for posterity. Victor's feet were clad in pink slippers. Strange, thought Madame Koska. Why is he wearing the slippers? Didn't M. Danilov tell her that Victor was practising dancing barefoot, to get into the habit for the innovative new ballets, starting with *Icarus*? No, of course he would wear the slippers for this occasion. They were part of the classic *Spectre* costume... This is how he would want it to appear.

Suddenly, Victor looked around. "Where is Galina?" he asked.

"Galina is in Switzerland," said M. Danilov. "You know she had been ill for a while and needed to go to a sanatorium."

"Yes, I know," said Victor, somewhat agitated. "But I thought she would dance one last *Spectre* with me, for the film, so posterity can see her."

"No, no, my boy, she cannot," said the impresario, kindly.

"You will be dancing with me, Victor," said Lavrova sharply. "It will be the best *Spectre* you have ever danced."

"With you?" said Victor softly. "But...we never danced *Spectre* together."

"We will now," said the ballerina brusquely. "And everyone will love it. Lavrova and Parizhsky, their first *Le Spectre de la Rose* together, for future generations."

Victor stood motionless for a minute. His big black eyes were thoughtful, assessing the new situation.

"Very well," he said. "We will dance, of course. But Sasha, I must go for a minute to my dressing room. I forgot to take one of my medications, and the doctor said they keep me strong if I wish to dance."

"Don't delay too long," said M. Danilov. "The crew will want to start filming very soon."

"No, it won't take any time, Sasha. I just want to swallow this medicine."

It took about ten minutes for him to come back. Danilov and Lavrova seemed annoyed. The film crew left the stage and went further into the darkness where their equipment was waiting. Madame Koska left the stage and settled at the front row, ready to watch.

Finally Victor reappeared on the stage and went to Danilov and Lavrova. "I am ready," he said. Danilov motioned him to take his place behind the opened "window" in the wings. Lavrova followed him. The orchestra began to play the short introduction, and Madame Koska suddenly realised that Victor was not wearing his slippers. What could that mean? She wondered. First, he wore them, then he did not…strange. But how can it be significant in any way, and who is telling him when to wear them and when not to? Did he suddenly remember that he wanted to practise dancing in bare feet? Surely this occasion was not one for experiments?

Suddenly, in a flash, Madame Koska knew exactly how Solange died, in every little detail. All the pieces fell into place and the scenario of the murder became so clear that Madame Koska could not believe that she had not seen it long ago. But could she prove it? Who would believe it unless it happened again? And in a second wave of shock and horror, Madame Koska knew it was about to happen, right there in front of her. But she was helpless to act—she had to wait, in agonising tension, for the first indication.

The young girl caressed and dropped her rose on the floor and sank into her chair, falling asleep. The Spectre leapt from the window, light as a feather, landing softly on the stage and dancing around the sleeping girl. Madame Koska felt a tight knot in her stomach and her throat became dry and constricted. It was almost the end of the performance. The Spectre kissed the sleeping girl, and in a few seconds he would make the final leap through another "window." After that, the girl would wake up and pick up the rose. And Madame Koska saw the Spectre do a tiny, but incongruous move with his foot.

Madame Koska jumped to her feet and screamed, "Stop the show! Stop the filming! Tanya, don't touch the rose!" The whole company present froze in their seats, and Victor turned to Madame Koska and smiled. "How clever of you, Madame Koska!"

Madame Koska could not talk. She could hardly breathe. Her throat was entirely shut and she was trembling all over.

"What the hell is going on?" said Danilov, looking at Madame Koska as if she had lost her mind. "Why are you doing this? Do you realise how much it will cost?"

"At least it won't cost the life of Tanya Lavrova," said Madame Koska, recovering her voice. As always when terribly upset, she forgot to change her W's into V's. At that moment, Inspector Blount advanced from the dark back of the theatre with another policeman. They walked on stage and stood near Victor, who was gazing at them with mild surprise. "Where did you come from?" he asked the inspector.

"Victor Parizhsky, I am arresting you for the murder of Solange Forestier," said Inspector Blount. "You do not have to say anything, but it may harm your defence if you do not mention when questioned something which you later…"

"Wait a minute, Inspector, please," interrupted Madame Koska. "Let me talk to him."

"But we have to stay next to you, Madame Koska," said the inspector. "I am about to arrest him."

"Of course," said Madame Koska. "But you know he is not dangerous to any of us. Let me just speak to him for a few moments."

"Very well," said the inspector. Madame Koska turned to Victor who was standing placidly, not saying anything. M. Danilov was standing a short distance away, seemingly too shocked to say or do anything.

"My dear boy," said Madame Koska softly. "You really must tell me why you killed Solange."

"Oh, you know about Solange?" said Victor, surprised. "I thought no one knew."

"Yes, I know," said Madame Koska. "And you must tell me because everyone thinks Madame Danilova killed her."

"What?" cried Victor, his face turning bright red. "Why would they think that? No, I killed her! Galina is a saint, she would never hurt anyone!"

"You love her very much?" asked Madame Koska.

"She is like a mother to me," said Victor, now sobbing openly. "She is the only one in the world who understands me. She is an angel, a fairy, a pure spirit!"

"So you killed Solange for her?" asked Madame Koska.

"Yes. Sasha wanted to replace Galina. He thought she was getting older, and he wanted a young girl to take her place. I could not allow that. I knew Galina would suffer if she could not dance."

"But you know this was not the case at all, don't you? You know the truth is that Galina is sick with tuberculosis, and had to go to get the cure?"

"I did not know it then... I only found out after I had killed Solange, and then when I realised my mistake, everything went black, just a huge black pool, and I fainted, and when I woke up, I was at the hospital. I don't remember much of what happened in between, Madame."

"So how did you kill her? I don't want to hurt you, my dear, but if I don't know the details, they may never believe it, and they may keep Galina in jail forever, or maybe even execute her."

Victor started trembling, his face white and strained. "I will tell you everything, Madame Koska. Everything. Just make sure that they don't hurt Galina. I'd much rather they execute me."

"They will not do so, my dear. You are not well, you will have to stay some time in a nice hospital, and be taken care of, but no one will hurt you, I promise."

"But I will never dance again, will I?"

"I don't know, Victor. Do you want to dance?"

"Yes, I want to dance. That is all I want in the world. But I will accept it as my punishment. You know I fly, don't you? When I do the grand jeté, or any elevation, I don't fall to earth like other people?"

"Yes, I know that. When I saw you rehearsing for *Icarus*, wearing these wings, I knew you could fly."

"Icarus," said Victor thoughtfully. "His wings were clipped. Mine will be clipped, too. I deserve the punishment." He put his head in his hands and seemed to drift into another world.

Madame Koska stroked his hair gently. Poor Icarus, she thought. Poor, insane boy. He will never fly into the sun again.

"Now tell me everything," she said, pressing his hand. "We must save Galina."

"I could not stand it. I was so confused, my mind felt on fire. I kept seeing these big dark eyes looking at me from everywhere, and I was hearing voices that told me to save Galina's place. I had to kill Solange. I thought if I killed her, Galina would not be banished."

"So how did you kill her? You were on stage with her all the time!" said Madame Koska. The young man looked at her with agonised eyes. It was as if they were entirely alone—the people around them were silent.

"I had a vial of poison which I had kept for years. You see, I had been thinking, on and off, about suicide. When I became a great success, I forgot about it, but when I wanted to kill Solange I remembered it."

"And it never occurred to you that once Solange was gone, M. Danilov would find another dancer?"

"No, I was not thinking very clearly. I just knew I had to kill her. I thought about the plan carefully, though. It involved the silk roses. You know, there is a rose that the girl brings from the ball, it falls to the floor when she sleeps, and she picks it up and smells it at the end of the dance. If that rose could be poisoned, I would accomplish the murder on stage, and no one would suspect me. So, I had to find a way to substitute a poisoned rose that the girl would pick up. During the dance, some petals and a few roses always fall to the floor, so if I kept one silk rose from a previous performance, while the others were removed to be reattached to the costume, I could poison it. I attached it, loosely, to my arm band, tied with a bow. All I had to do was pull on the string, and the rose would fall on the floor."

Madame Koska looked at Madame Lavrova. This was the exact way she had advised Natalya and Gretchen to attach the roses to the silk hat...a stage trick. Lavrova nodded, understanding the question in Madame Koska's eyes. The great ballerina was crying silently and Madame Koska felt for her.

The inspector looked at Madame Koska. "But how could he exchange the roses?" he asked. "The whole audience would see him bend down to do so."

"That is why he danced barefoot, Inspector. Madame Danilova revealed to me that his secret for the long 'flights' when he was doing the grand jeté was that his toes were exceptionally strong. He would land on his toes instead of on the ball of the foot, like other male dancers do, almost as if he had toe shoes and danced en pointe. While performing the complex pirouettes, circling around the sleeping girl, he used his strong toes to pick up and place the clean rose under the chair, then used his toes again to pick up and put the poisoned rose at the exact place the girl was expecting to find it at the end of the dance."

Victor looked at her with vague admiration. "You are so clever, Madame Koska. Yes, Galina told me I could trust you."

Trust me to find out you are a murderer, poor boy, thought Madame Koska. Trust me to have you locked up for life in an insane asylum. Trust me to clip your wings... But what can one do? He did murder, and he would murder again if he could. Madame Koska sighed. "Where is the poison, Victor?" she asked.

"In my dressing room. When Sasha told me I had to dance with Madame Lavrova, I hated her so much for taking Galina's place that I knew I had to kill her, too, and this was my opportunity. So I went back to my dressing room, attached a rose to my armband, poisoned it, and removed my slippers."

Lavrova moved closer to look at Victor. She was sobbing openly. "I am so sorry, Madame Lavrova," said Madame Koska. "I had no idea you liked Victor so much... Or is it nerves because of his attempt on your life?"

"No," said the ballerina. "Like Victor? No, I don't like this miserable little madman at all, nor do I have nerves or worry about my escape. I am crying because of the huge loss for the world of ballet. The film of Lavrova and Parizhsky will not be finished... Posterity will not have it as a treasure."

"For heaven's sake," said Madame Koska, irritated and amazed. "Solange was killed, you were almost poisoned, a man goes insane, and that is all that worries you?"

"All? That is the only thing, Madame Koska. Only the ballet matters. We are nothing...just small parts of the huge entity of the arts. You will not understand it, but Sasha would. Please, please, Madame Koska, let us finish the filming. Let us have the film for posterity, it really is the only important matter here."

Madame Koska looked at M. Danilov. He came forward and took Lavrova's hand in his. "Yes, I agree, Tanya. Please, Madame Koska, Inspector Blount, let us finish the filming."

Victor looked at them mildly. "What do you mean? Of course we must finish the filming. Why not?"

Inspector Blount looked as if he were in the midst of an insane asylum. "What do you mean, you want to finish the filming? We have a murderer here, who should be arrested!"

"Inspector," said Madame Koska, regaining her calm enough to remember her Vs and Ws. "He can't escape. The last giant leap through the vindow takes him into the arms of four men who stand there to catch him and cover him vith varm towels. Send the police officer to stand vith them and all vill be in order."

"And what about the poisoned rose?" asked the inspector. "You can't tell me you will allow Madame Lavrova to smell any rose from the floor of this stage?"

"We will remove that rose for police inspection," said Madame Koska, "and I will give Madame Lavrova a similar rose; I have one attached to my hat, Inspector."

"You brought a rose with you?" asked the inspector, surprised. "Why?"

"Just a hunch, Inspector Blount. Just a hunch it vould be needed."

"Very well," said the inspector, looking at Madame Koska with mixed incredulity and admiration. "Tomorrow morning I will think I had lost my mind for agreeing, but never mind. Go ahead, M. Danilov. Finish the film."

M. Danilov sprang to life and started giving instructions. Lavrova returned to her chair. The poisoned rose was carefully put in a bag by the police officer, and Madame Koska's rose was put on the freshly swept floor. The film crew, who had been standing wordlessly around, returned to their equipment. And Victor stepped into the spot he was about to occupy before taking the giant leap.

"Go!" said M. Danilov. The orchestra started playing, the film crew started filming. Victor took four great steps to the window and leapt into the air, soaring like a glorious bird, and out of the dark window into the wings, which looked like a magical, deep blue night.

Madame Koska did not remain for the end of the show; she did not want to see Victor arrested officially and taken away. She did not want to talk to anyone from the ballet, not at that moment. Of course, she would have to speak and work with M. Danilov, Lavrova, Bassin... But she could not face Danilov's obsession, Lavrova's heartlessness, and Bassin's stupidity. Nor did she wish to speak with Inspector Blount. Yes, she was glad he had come, but she needed to get away from him for a while. She moved swiftly to a side door next to the stage and saw Mr. Korolenko waiting for her. They quickly left the theatre, and Mr. Korolenko said, "I was waiting in the back."

"I am glad to see you... I feel like an executioner. He is insane, Dmitry. He does not know what he does...and his great talent is now going to disappear forever."

"There was no choice, Vera. He is extremely dangerous. He really does not understand the horror of his crimes, but you do. He cannot be allowed freedom."

"Yes, and he knows it. There will never be another Victor Parizhsky, Dmitry. Never."

"I know. But he will be remembered forever. He will not be forgotten, and his name will be legend."

"And the myths about his flying will just grow," said Madame Koska. "How sad Galina is going to be." She touched her handkerchief to her eyes.

"Vera, you need a vacation. You need to get away. I have to go abroad soon to meet some people in Germany about book translations. How would you like to come with me?"

"But I am so busy..."

"You can do it after you finish the *Icarus* costumes. The summer, you told me, is always less busy at any atelier. Or do you think it will cause eyebrows to be raised? If so, you can marry me before we go, you know. Easy enough."

Madame Koska laughed. "No, no. No one will raise an eyebrow... This is the twentieth century! One doesn't have to marry just to go on vacation."

"I would not mind marrying you," said Mr. Korolenko generously, as if bestowing a great favour. Madame Koska smiled and took his arm.

"No, no marriage. At least not yet, Dmitry. But yes, I'd love to go to Germany with you. Also, you know, I have heard a lot about these new entertainment spots, the cabarets. They are most important in Berlin."

"The cabarets? But they are risqué! Inappropriate! Vulgar!" said Mr. Korolenko, surprised.

"You know much about them?" asked Madame Koska.

"I know the owner of one in Berlin," said Mr. Korolenko. "He is a Hungarian. An interesting character."

"You know everyone everywhere," said Madame Koska.

"Well, yes, I know a lot of people, some not so respectable," admitted Mr. Korolenko. "But why do you need to see a cabaret?"

"I have a hunch that their styles are going to grow into society fashion, and that the whole concept will be important to the atelier. I might as well learn about it from the start."

"Another hunch..." said Mr. Korolenko, smiling. "Well, let's stop for coffee, shall we, before we get back to work?"